MURDER AT THE SEASIDE HOTEL: A 1920S HISTORICAL COZY MYSTERY

AN EVIE PARKER MYSTERY BOOK 5

SONIA PARIN

ISBN: 9781695696426

CHAPTER 1

Oh, those seaside trippers, oh, those seaside trippers.
Up and down they gaily go, where the breeze is blowing. -
Will Terry "Seaside Trippers" 1914 song

Summer, 1920
Worthing, England

"*M*ilady, it's time to wake up."

"But I only just closed my eyes." Evie threw a pillow over her face. "Come back in half an hour."

"You have been asleep for two whole hours and you were quite firm about me waking you up now because you only needed a brief rest."

"Two hours? Surely not. I must say, I cannot recommend this hotel for its peace and quiet," Evie grumbled.

Caro continued, her tone light and cheerful, "I honestly can't understand why you would wish to miss out on such a splendid day. Edmonds and I have strolled along the Pavilion pier several times. Everyone is out and about enjoying themselves. I have just pressed your lovely dress and Tom has been pacing."

Evie lifted the pillow and peered at Caro. "You're going to keep talking until I get up."

Caro gave her a bright smile. "Yes. That is the plan. You might not be excited, but this is my first trip to the seaside and I aim to make the best of it. Everyone has been so lovely and friendly. Of course, no one can tell I am a lady's maid or maybe everyone is simply too happy to be by the seaside to notice or even care that they might be rubbing shoulders with a maid. The air alone is enough to make me smile. The sooner you get up, the sooner I can get on with enjoying the rest of the day… I hope you don't think I am speaking out of turn, but you did give me leave to use any means possible to wake you up."

Sighing, Evie flung the bedcovers off. "Happy now?"

"Oh, yes. Although, I was happy before. I suppose that means I am even happier now. I believe Tom has planned an outing for you or maybe an afternoon tea. I'm not sure which. If you were to ask him, he would tell you he's had plenty of time to change his mind while you slept the afternoon away. Anyhow, Edmonds has an outing planned for us. Did you know the first moving picture show in Worthing was seen on the pier way back in 1896? I didn't know that. Here's another fact…"

Evie yawned. "Is it about the pier? If it is, I'm not sure I want to hear about it."

"No, it's about the Midsummer Tree. It stands near Broadwater Green and is said to be around 300 years old. Can you believe that? Some people still believe skeletons rise from the tree and dance around it until dawn on Midsummer's Eve. We're close enough to the date. Do you think we might see them? I hope we do."

Hugging the pillow against her, Evie croaked, "You're determined to ensure I don't curl up and fall asleep again."

Caro gave the pillow a tug. "I don't understand why you are so tired. It's not as if we drove all the way from Berkshire."

"I find traveling from one place to another tiring." Releasing her hold on the pillow, Evie stretched. "Fine. I'm awake and I am up. Is your room suitable?"

"Oh, yes. It actually has a view."

"Why are you surprised?"

Caro shrugged and busied herself straightening a cushion on the chaise longue at the foot of the bed.

Understanding dawned. A lady's maid was usually allocated a room somewhere in the attics or in the back of the house. But this was as much Caro's vacation as it was Evie's.

"When we returned from our promenade, Edmonds said he wished to go to his room so he could enjoy his view. He is ever so grateful you decided to bring him along too."

3

"Yes, well... There was no talking Tom out of driving the roadster and we couldn't fit all the luggage in there because that would have left no room for you. Now that I think about it, I believe he planned it this way all along since the only way he could drive the roadster was if the larger motor car could carry the extra gasoline."

Caro inspected the hat she had selected for Evie to wear. "I felt like a grand lady traveling with my very own chauffeur in the *Duesenberg*. I have been meaning to ask..."

When Caro hesitated, Evie smiled. "Do feel free to do so. What's on your mind?"

"I know you mentioned wanting to celebrate our ten-year anniversary, but I can't help wondering... You didn't seem awfully keen to travel..."

Evie gave it some thought. Her granny's so-called surprise visit had been delayed by Toodles' desire to visit Venice. Evie had made all the preparations for her arrival, exhausting her household staff until she thought everything would be perfect and now all that hard work would have to be postponed for the time being. "I think everyone needs a break from me. The timing is perfect."

In reality, she would have thoroughly enjoyed staying at Halton House where it was nice and cozy, in a grand sort of manner.

However, she had received an invitation from the hotel owner and, most importantly, she had realized her maid had been with her for ten years. Evie had surprised Caro by remarking upon the upcoming event and suggesting they do something to celebrate it.

While Caro had not understood the significance or Evie's excitement, Evie had been unable to ignore it. Caro had been her first personal maid and she had become quite attached to the young woman's company.

It had taken some doing to find out what Caro wanted and she had only succeeded because her other maid, Millicent, had forced the information out of her.

Caro had never been to the seaside and she had claimed she would like nothing better than to spend a few days there, preferably staying somewhere with a pretty view.

If Caro had asked to be presented to the Prince of Wales, Evie would have stopped at nothing to make it happen for her. A trip to the seaside had been such a small dream to Evie... Then again, she had grown up in Newport, Rhode Island, so the sea didn't hold the same novelty.

Despite having their destination settled by the timely and generous offer Evie had received from the owner of the hotel, she'd then had to tie up some loose ends. Before setting off, there had been a round of scheduled visits to take care of, committee meetings to attend, as well as some last-minute meetings with the estate manager and the trustees looking after the current Earl's welfare. Evie had spent a week rushing around and now felt she needed a week to recuperate.

If only she could...

If she spent all her vacation time in bed or lounging about, Evie knew Caro would worry about her so she really needed to make an effort and get into the spirit of it all. At least, for Caro's sake…

"Why don't you go ahead and join Edmonds. I can dress myself. Oh, and make sure Tom doesn't wear out the carpet with his pacing. Actually, where is he doing his pacing?"

"It's not just pacing, milady. He is brooding and he's doing it in public, in the lobby."

That struck Evie as odd. Tom had been only too happy to set off on their trip to the seaside. "What could have come over him?"

"If you ask me, he's craving some excitement," Caro suggested.

"Impossible. He's always trying to talk me out of becoming involved in things that shouldn't concern me." Evie stilled and stared out of the window. "Heavens, I believe I just made myself sound like a busybody."

Caro rummaged through Evie's luggage and produced another hat. "I think this one will suit you best with that dress. It has cherries on it."

Evie glanced at the hat. Cherries? What had she been thinking? "Yes, that will do very nicely, thank you. Run along now, Caro. Don't let my tardiness spoil your vacation."

Caro laughed. "If any of the maids working here heard you, they'd clobber me over the head just to steal my job away from me."

"Well, let's hope it doesn't come to that."

CHAPTER 2

*E*vie walked down the central staircase casting an appreciative glance at the seascapes displayed along the way.

The Hotel St. James had, until recently, been a private seaside home. The previous owners had been prominent members of society with a knighthood here and there, but they had fallen on hard times when successive heirs had died, with the most recent heir running up such vast debts he had been forced to sell the house. Although, according to rumors, he had lost the house at cards.

A forward-thinking entrepreneur had purchased the property and had decided to turn it into a luxury hotel for the well to-do. The fact Evie had requested rooms with views for her maid and chauffeur had at first been frowned upon by the manager. But a word with the owner had sorted it all out. After all, he had extended the invitation.

When Evie had told the dowager about it, Henrietta had been somewhat suspicious of the offer...

"I believe he wishes to gain your seal of approval," Henrietta had said.

New money, the dowager had then remarked, was beginning to make some people more prominent but not entirely visible or acceptable within certain circles.

While they were financially on the rise, they remained quite insignificant and inconspicuous because even large fortunes did not buy them a place in society which was where one could come to know the right people. If only they could gain access.

Evie had wanted to know if this so-called society had a particular meeting place only to realize the dowager had been referring to the grand houses and families living in them. She supposed that included herself and... just about everyone she knew. Something she found amusing since, in reality, Evie belonged to the new money set.

As for Evie wishing to give her maid a vacation...

Henrietta had lifted her eyebrows, but she had refrained from commenting. Anyone else in her position would have made a point of instructing Evie on the ways of their world and the differences between servants and... the rest of them.

Then again, the dowager took great pride in always being the exception, accepting Evie into the family, embracing her odd ways and even celebrating them.

Evie smiled. It had all worked out well in the end and they were bound to spend a glorious week by the seaside...

Despite the initial glitch with the hotel manager, Mr. Rudy Moorhouse, the hotel owner, had been only too happy to organize a premier room for Caro, assuring Evie he would make all the necessary arrangements. Evie had been prepared to cover the extra costs of providing her maid with a well-appointed room but Mr. Rudy Moorhouse had been eager to waive it.

"Mark my word," Henrietta had warned, "he is determined to use you. Word about you staying at the hotel will spread and people will want to follow suit. You will be setting a trend for him. You know nothing about his background, so you risk associating yourself with who knows what type of scoundrel…"

It didn't bother Evie. Being as rich as *Croesus*, she had the means to travel anywhere she wished, but she had seen no reason to look a gift horse in the mouth.

Evie glanced around the lobby taking in the fashionable style and wondered if Mr. Moorhouse would prove the dowager correct. His taste certainly couldn't be faulted, she thought. No one would criticize the chairs upholstered in sea green or the rest of the decorations, mostly small bronze statues and paintings of seascapes. Nothing she or anyone could find offensive, Evie thought.

When she reached the bottom of the stairs, Evie saw Tom sitting on a curved sofa flanked by palm trees. A woman stood behind him, partially hidden by a statue of a turbaned gentleman and she appeared to be studying Tom. Evie didn't blame her. Tom Winchester, the bodyguard her granny had hired to make sure Evie didn't fall prey to some unscrupulous gold-digger or kidnapper, had the sort of appealing looks that made him stand out in a crowd.

Seeing her, Tom jumped to his feet and made a beeline for her. "I thought I might have to go up to make sure you hadn't been kidnapped or murdered in your sleep."

"What nonsense. Who would want to kidnap me? I would make such a fuss, they would release me in no time."

"That, I believe."

"Now, what do you have planned for us? Caro mentioned something about an afternoon tea."

Tom nodded. "Right after we visit the pier. Caro hasn't stopped talking about it all day. By the way, nice hat."

"Thank you. I'm afraid it's one of those impulse decisions I am currently regretting." Ever since abandoning her pretty floral prints in favor of the more fashionable blocks of color, she had been feeling bereft of... well, she supposed she missed the distraction afforded by floral patterns. Evie laughed. "In case you are wondering, I'm prattling on in silence about my fashion choices when I know I should be asking you why you have been pacing."

Tom gave her a casual shrug and led her out of the hotel. "Perhaps it has something to do with the fact the roadster can do more than sixty miles per hour and yet this trip took two days to complete."

Evie didn't bother hiding her surprise. "You wanted to drive faster?"

He tipped his hat down and lowered his voice to a murmur. "At least a little bit faster."

"Where's the joy in that? You miss out on the scenery when it all becomes a blur."

His eyes twinkled. "Ah, yes, but you get to enjoy driving a fast car."

"You call that an argument?" Evie gave an unlady-like snort. "Think of all the pretty villages we discovered along the way. Besides, you know how Henrietta feels about driving too fast. Since hearing about our trip, she has related numerous stories about the motor car accidents she has been hearing about."

Tom made a point of looking over his shoulder. "I don't see the dowager anywhere."

"And just as well. Henrietta didn't see the point of traveling all this way just to look at the sea. One glance at it and she would have insisted we return." Evie exchanged smiles with a couple walking by. "I believe this is going to be an extraordinarily dull vacation. Think about it. We have traveled all the way from Berkshire to Sussex without a single mishap delaying our journey. Although, you might argue that point by complaining we didn't need to stop overnight along the way. Anyhow, I think we are experiencing a quiet lull. Anything might have happened, but it didn't."

"You almost sounded wistful just then. Are you, by any chance, missing your days of murder and mayhem?"

Oh... Yes, she had sounded rather nostalgic! "Of course, not. Perhaps I need to use this vacation to become accustomed to a more humdrum existence. After all, it's what I have been craving all along."

Looking at the people strolling along, Evie decided Caro had been right. Everyone looked cheerful and carefree. "Say something amusing, Tom. I feel the need to join in the fun. Or, at least, appear to be enjoying myself."

Tom looked up at the sky. "I think the seagulls are finding your hat rather attractive. Look, they're hovering above you and I swear they are eyeing the cherries on your hat."

Evie laughed. "You tease me. Oh… *Heavens!*"

A seagull swooped down.

Tom grabbed her arm and drew Evie away from the seagull's path just in time to avoid it. "Keep your head down and hold onto your hat. Or, better still, sacrifice it. Give the seagull what it wants."

"Do you think we should turn back?"

"No, I think I can defend you against a few squawking seagulls."

Evie's voice hitched. "There are more?"

Putting his hand on her hat, Tom suggested taking cover in a tea room.

To the amusement of some onlookers, they broke into a run with Evie squealing, "I can't see where we're going."

"Mind your step."

Evie lifted her foot in time to avoid tripping over the step leading into the tea room.

"I think we're safe now," Tom said.

"Well, thank goodness for that." Evie adjusted her

hat. "I would hate to be asked to leave because I've arrived accompanied by a flock of enraged seagulls."

Glancing at the tables set up outside the tea room in the open air, Tom said, "As inviting as they look, I think we would be asking for trouble if we requested to be seated out here. Let's play it safe and go inside. We can watch the world go by from the safety of a table by the window." He guided her inside the tea room and said, "I see a couple of guests from the hotel. I suppose that is a commendation of sorts."

"Oh, who? Where?"

"The lady with a hat similar to yours. Perhaps she too is taking shelter here."

"More cherries? I shall have to burn this hat." Her gaze skated over the tables until she spotted a woman wearing a straw hat. "I don't think they're cherries. They look more like strawberries." Evie thought the gentleman sitting beside her looked familiar. "I think I saw them when we arrived this morning. Or perhaps I only saw him. Yes, he was in the lobby reading a newspaper. I remember noticing the tilt of his hat and thinking he looked like a *bon vivant* but now I'm not so sure."

"May I ask why you changed your mind about him?"

"He looks rather displeased about something. Look at him. He's drumming his fingers on the table. Then again, I'm told you were pacing earlier on and you're not exactly the pacing type. Or, at least, I didn't think you were. Perhaps they've been made to wait too long for their tea. Although, his companion looks rather pleased with herself." On closer inspection, Evie thought her smile looked a little forced. She might even go so far as to say the woman looked somewhat downcast, but she didn't mention it.

Since Caro had only noticed people being happy, Evie decided she should put in an effort.

They were shown through to a table by the window and Evie made sure to shift her chair slightly so she could study the hotel guests.

Tom laughed.

"Do share," Evie invited.

"I'm thinking about your remark. You're quite right about me pacing. I had been feeling jumpy. I went through a cycle of picking up a newspaper, setting it down, pacing around, sitting down again... But nothing held my interest for long until I found an article about... Well, never mind that. And now you are thoroughly intrigued by the hotel guests. What does that tell you about us?"

Evie straightened. "Oh. Oh, my. Are we missing the exhilaration of a murder mystery? And I'm not referring to the play we were recently forced to take part in."

"There's something to be said for puzzles," Tom said. "They have certainly kept us engaged."

"Well, we can't become embroiled in a murder mystery here," Evie said. "For starters, what are the chances of someone being killed? Also, we don't have access to our resourceful library." Evie gave him a whimsical smile. "Although, that wouldn't necessarily stop us. I am, after all, a Countess."

"Meaning?"

"I could gain entry into a grand house to access their library."

Tom tipped his head back and laughed. "That should put any prospective killer on notice."

"I should think so." Picking up the menu, Evie wondered about the local constabulary. Not that she would have cause to liaise with the police whilst on vacation. She hummed under her breath and raised the menu slightly to hide her smile.

Glancing at Evie, Tom said, "I can see you smiling but I can't quite figure out what you find amusing."

"Oh, nothing."

A waiter, sporting a thin moustache and dressed in a white jacket and black trousers, stood by ready to take their orders.

"I feel we should celebrate our vacation with a decadent glass of champagne but I fear I might fall asleep." She settled for tea and sandwiches and smiled as Tom ordered extra roast beef sandwiches.

"You always take a nibble of your favorite cucumber sandwiches," he said, "and then devour all the roast beef ones."

Smiling, Evie turned her attention to the view of the sea. "I suppose we should take note of everything we see. Henrietta will want a full report. Oh, look. I think that's Caro and Edmonds emerging from the Pavilion. Now she is heading back in... She must really like it. We might have to see what all the fuss is about."

"It's a promenade deck. What's there to see?"

"She seemed to be quite happy to see people... being

happy. Now I'm thinking she would be beside herself with happiness if she crossed the Atlantic. During the last voyage over here, I noticed people were forever saying they were off to take a promenade around the ship. I hope she's collecting plenty of stories. She could be our source of information."

"Is this about Henrietta questioning your decision to come to Worthing?"

"I believe she has made me determined to appreciate the waves rolling in. And, who knows, we might see something of real interest. We should go for a drive around the area or venture out to the nearby villages." Lowering her voice, she asked, "Are the hotel guests any happier?"

After a moment, Tom said, "They have been served their tea but I don't see them conversing. I'd hate to say it but they might have had a spat."

"That would be in poor taste. Think of the sour memories they will take home with them." Brightening, Evie said, "What do you think you can tell me about them?"

"Is this a game?" Tom asked.

It could be, Evie thought. "They're staying at the same hotel so we are bound to cross paths. Eventually, we'll learn everything there is to know about them. I think it would be fun to try to guess something about them now."

Shifting slightly, Tom studied them. "They're not newlyweds. That's my first observation."

"I'm inclined to agree with you." Evie stole a glance and, noticing the woman's smile did not reach her eyes, she decided to revise her first impression of her. She actually looked quite unhappy. "If they are newlyweds, it's quite possible she married against her wishes or vice versa. Or... now that they are married, he has told her the truth about his fortune. Alas, there isn't one so they will have to live off her inheritance."

Tom took a moment to think about it. "I'm going to have to disagree. She doesn't look that unhappy. If he had lied about his fortune, I believe she would be back in the hotel packing her suitcases."

"You are easily fooled, Mr. Winchester. I suggest you take a closer look at her eyes. They're not sparkling."

"Do you think she is pretending to be happy?" Tom asked.

"Yes. And that is not so unusual. I've been known to put up a brave front." Evie smiled at the waiter as he set their tea on the table. Changing the subject, she said, "Tom, I'm going to need your assistance. I don't wish to spoil Caro's time here so you will have to help me enjoy myself. She said you had some activities planned..."

"Well, there's the pier."

Evie took a sip of her tea. They were booked into the hotel for a week. Just how many times could they enjoy a promenade along the pier?

"There are some interesting Stone Age flint mines in the area," Tom continued. "The most significant site is called the *Cissbury Ring*." Tom tipped his head back in thought. "Augustus Lane-Fox excavated part of it back in 1867..."

"Tom."

"Yes?"

"Can you think of something other than the pier and a flint mine?"

"We should visit the Worthing Museum, as well as the library. Andrew Carnegie funded the library."

Evie perked up. "Oh, there is a library!"

Helping himself to some tea, Tom mused, "I'm not quite sure how to interpret your enthusiasm."

Sighing, Evie said, "I suppose I might be missing the comforts of home. Ever since settling at Halton House, I have been meaning to breathe easy and relax. I know the need is contrary to what everyone else is doing." It had been nearly two years since the Great War had ended and everyone seemed to be intent on enjoying as much of life as they could. In all honesty, Evie had never thought she would become the type of person who enjoyed spending afternoons curled up in the library with a book...

Then again... Lately, the library had become quite resourceful, providing them with relevant information to assist the police with a couple of incidents.

Suddenly, she understood Tom's amusement at her interest in the local library.

Evie perked up. "Oh, another couple just came in and I think I recognize them from the hotel."

"A timely arrival," Tom mused, "providing you with an excuse to change the subject."

"Not really since we can now continue our game."

Tom took a discreet peek at the new arrivals. "He's a

banker. Mr. Hector Addington and that is his wife, Mrs. Addington."

"I take it you have met them."

"No, I overheard a conservation."

"While you were pacing or brooding?" Evie asked.

"I can't be sure. I only remember hearing them say they were making their way to a restaurant for luncheon." The edge of his lip kicked up. "Oh, look. She is wearing a hat just like yours."

Evie made sure to sound offended when she said, "It is nothing like mine. Those are plums, I'm sure." Evie studied Mrs. Addington. "She looks extremely pleased with herself and he looks quite proud to have her by his side."

"Newlyweds?" Tom asked.

"Yes. They appear to only have eyes for each other." Trying to be as inconspicuous as possible, Evie continued watching them as they settled down at their table. "She is almost bouncing in her chair. I doubt I have ever seen eyes shining so brightly." Or cheeks so flushed with excitement, Evie thought. Although, the woman might have been a little heavy-handed with the rouge… "That is a look of triumph."

"Over what?" Tom asked.

Giving a small shrug, Evie said, "Perhaps his family did not approve of her and she managed to change their minds or maybe he went ahead and married her without their approval."

"Are men in high society likely to do that?"

"It would take a special type of man," Evie said, "one

brave enough to go against family expectations and everything that is socially acceptable."

"And you think a banker would possess such a rebellious character trait?"

"Perhaps not. Are you sure he's a banker? The only ones I have ever encountered have been rather stuffy, disapproving and gray haired." Nibbling on a sandwich, Evie wondered if Mr. Addington might have been forced into banking by his family. "Now I think she looks far too happy."

Tom's eyebrows rose a notch. "Is there something wrong with that?"

Evie tried to formulate a response that wouldn't come across as snobbish. "These might be modern times, but certain modes of behavior continue to be highly regarded as the acceptable standard."

Now Tom looked confused. "What exactly does that mean?"

"Well, there is being happy and then there is being ostentatiously happy."

"One is good and the other isn't?" he asked, "I had no idea happiness could only be expressed by measured degrees. So how would you describe Mrs. Addington's state of happiness?"

"Oh, I'm not the one doing the measuring or censorship."

"I see. This is one of those unwritten social rules."

Evie gave a small nod of agreement.

"And you don't want to spell it out for me. Fine. I'll take a guess and say it's something to do with taste.

Perhaps a fine line drawn between boorish behavior and graceful conduct whilst in public."

Evie grinned. "Henrietta would be proud of you."

"So, what does that tell us about Mrs. Addington?"

The young woman hadn't quite learned the rules of behavior in polite society, Evie thought.

"That the person she is pretending to be does not come naturally to her. It reminds me of poor Mrs. Hemsworth. She was actually quite wealthy but she hailed from the Midwest and, when she arrived in Newport, she pretended to be from Boston. Everyone could tell straightaway. Ordinarily, she would have been snubbed by the society matrons but she had this quaint giggle everyone admired so they tolerated everything else about her. Also, she donated a great deal of money to the local library."

"Why would she pretend to be someone she is not?" Tom asked.

"She might hail from what we refer to as the wrong side of the tracks. For all we know, she might be a chorus girl."

"And that's why his family would have disapproved of her?"

"Precisely. Clearly, he is a man in love, willing to turn his back on his family for the sake of the woman who has captured his heart." Evie took a pensive sip of her tea. "Being in banking, he must be well versed in calculated risks. I daresay, he knows where he stands with his family. He is probably the one everyone admires and so, he most likely knew they would eventually bend to his will." Evie straightened. "He is also the youngest of two or three children."

Tom didn't hide his surprise. "How did you come to that conclusion?"

"Something I read somewhere about the first-born son being conservative, while the younger child is the one everyone dotes on and can get away with quite a lot."

Tom smiled, "Well, Countess? How do you feel about your vacation now? Do you still think it will be a dull affair?"

Evie smiled. Tom had come a long way from calling her ma'am to using her title as a form of... Well, to Evie it almost sounded like an endearment.

"Perhaps it won't be so dull after all." Even if it involved creating their own entertainment.

Half an hour later, Evie sighed. "I suppose we should now tackle the pier."

CHAPTER 3

"Shall we continue our little guessing game while we enjoy our promenade along the pier?" Tom asked.

Looking up to make sure the coast was clear of seagulls, Evie said, "That might be asking for trouble but I am willing to risk it." She drew in a deep breath and thought there was definitely something to be said for a refreshing seaside breeze. Her mind felt clear and she could sense a lightness to her step.

Tom pointed to a gentleman gazing out to sea. "He is far from home and dwelling on memories that are fast fading."

"Oh, that sounds so sad," Evie exclaimed. "I'm going to say he is rather pleased with himself. He never thought he would get away with his crime, but it has been years and, so far, the police have not caught up with him."

Tom mused, "I believe you are fixating on the criminal mind."

Hadn't that been the whole point to their little game? "I don't see Caro anywhere on the pier. She and Edmonds must have moved on to afternoon tea."

Chuckling, Tom said, "I wouldn't be surprised if she then insists on taking another stroll along the pier."

What did Caro find so intriguing here? "Did she mention seeing boats or fish? Maybe she saw someone fall into the water…"

Tom didn't hold back his laughter. "You would settle for nothing short of someone drowning to make any time spent on the pier interesting? Should we be concerned about your state of mind?"

"Are you afraid I am exhibiting a morbid interest in killers?"

He thought about it for a moment. "You might be struggling to find a middle ground between utter boredom and the thrill of the chase."

Quite possibly, Evie thought. In which case, she should try to nip this growing obsession in the bud before it became a real concern.

Tom pointed to a couple standing at the end of the pier. "What do you think of that couple? I'll take the first stab and say they appear to be up to no good."

Evie studied them for a moment. Whenever someone drew close to them, they moved slightly away, almost as if they wished to maintain their privacy. "I should like to prove you wrong and say they are talking about their exciting plans for their upcoming trip to France. However, there is no point in denying how much more interesting it is to think they are vacationing with his great aunt who has been declaring she is at death's door for some time now. She is the type to bemoan the fact she has reached the end and will soon be departing this mortal coil. Meanwhile, he is eager to get his hands on the inheritance she has promised him but there appears to be no end in sight. He has now decided to expedite matters. His wife agrees. This is the fifth year they have had to vacation here because it is his great aunt's favorite spot. The wife would much rather relax in the Riviera. How do you think they will do away with her?"

"A pillow over her face while she sleeps," Tom suggested.

"That will make them the prime suspects. Remember, he is the sole heir."

He nodded in agreement. "They are cunning and desperate enough to bribe one of the maids to assist them, paying her a small fortune to kill his great aunt while they are out and about breathing the fresh sea air at the pier."

Evie tilted her head from side to side. "Yes, that's possible. The maid would have to be facing some sort of dire situation and be in desperate need of money. She'd also have to be brutally cold-blooded. If she is caught, her miserable past will come to light."

"We might be giving them too much credit," Tom said. "For all we know, they lack creativity and might resolve to push his great aunt down the stairs as they are making their way to dinner."

"People have been known to survive falls," Evie mused. "Remember, she has lasted the distance. That means, she might have the constitution of an ox." Evie twirled her parasol. "If Caro asks, could we tell her we discussed cloud formations? I wouldn't want her to know we have been delving into the evil machinations of greedy people."

"Clouds." Tom pushed back his hat and looked up at the sky. "Many artists have been captivated enough to paint pictures of them. But are they any different to the clouds we see in Berkshire?"

A couple stopped near them and exclaimed with excitement as they pointed out to sea.

"Perhaps we can tell her we played a game of spot the hats. I have now lost count of the number of ladies wearing straw hats adorned with a variety of fruits."

"Ah, but your hat is the only one with any real appeal. After all, you managed to entice a whole flock of seagulls."

"I don't dare stroll the length of the pier again. The seagulls have been eyeballing me the whole time and I sense they are getting restless. Let's head back to the hotel. I should change for dinner. I promise it will only take me an hour to prepare."

"You say that with so much confidence. Since it will only take me a fraction of the time, I will make the best of it and try to discover ways to entertain you. I fear you might be about to reach the end of your tether and this is only the first day of our stay here."

Their walk back to the hotel seemed to take twice as long as everyone appeared to have reached a general consensus, appointing that time in the afternoon as the perfect moment to return to their hotels and everyone seemed to be eager to appreciate as much of the sunshine and fresh air as possible, taking their time and, in the process, clogging up the sidewalk.

Tom whistled a tune under his breath, prompting Evie to remark, "The sea air seems to inspire joyful ditties."

"Yes," he said. "I saw a notice posted at the end of the pier announcing a night of music and dancing. If all else fails, we might want to lift our spirits with some music. I'm sure that will take your mind off this afternoon's macabre entertainment."

"You wish to return to the pier. Again?"

"It will be nighttime. That is bound to lend it an air of mystique."

Gasping, Evie said, "As well as the perfect opportunity for someone to commit a crime. I can just picture it. A man desperate to rid himself of his wife, pushes her into the crashing waves."

Tom laughed. "I see there is no shifting your attention away from murder."

"You must admit, we have been involved in more than our fair share of incidents." And, each time, she had tried to mind her own business...

"You were quite instrumental in assisting to solve a couple of those cases. It makes me wonder if that is a sign you might have missed your true calling."

"Are you suggesting I should have taken up a profession?" Evie wanted to laugh at the idea but she found it too intriguing.

Tom craned his neck.

"What do you see? Is someone else being attacked by seagulls?" Evie clutched her hat just in case.

"No, but there must be something going on up ahead. I see a crowd congregated…" Tom reached for her arm and stopped her. "A crowd has formed outside our hotel."

Evie noticed a few people rushing to cross the street while others stopped and stood on tiptoes. There were clusters of people on both sides of the street, all looking toward the hotel. Some were pointing. Others appeared to be gaping as if in shock.

She had spent the afternoon playing a morbid game of imagining the worst about people and suddenly her mind drew a blank. She couldn't for the life of her imagine what could be happening up ahead.

"Let's see if we can get any closer," Tom suggested.

With so many people milling about, they could only manage to move at a snail's pace.

"Do you see anything yet?" Evie asked.

"No. There are too many people to see properly."

"What are they doing?" Looking around them, Evie saw the sidewalk behind them had become congested with strollers coming to a stop.

"They're just standing… as if waiting for something to happen. I don't see much movement."

What could that mean? What could they be looking at?

Tom guided her to the edge of the sidewalk. Holding her by her elbow, he stepped onto the road. "We might be able to make some progress. Stick close to the curb."

"I'm not sure I want to see what's happening. I'm beginning to get a bad feeling about this." Evie pressed her hand to her throat. What if something bad had happened to someone? The sun had been rather strong. Once, she had forgotten to wear a hat and had nearly fainted from the heat. "I believe I am trying to mask my trepidation with common sense. What if a lady stepped out for a walk and didn't take a hat, or worse, what if she wore a hat similar to mine and the seagulls took a liking to it?"

"If it makes you feel any better, I had entertained the same idea. I guess we both feel the need to assure ourselves nothing bad has really happened."

She glanced at Tom in time to see him take a deep swallow. "What? You just saw something."

His voice carried a degree of concern when he said, "The police are here and they appear to be trying to contain the situation."

Evie looked around and saw people rushing from the pier and heading toward them. She guessed they had heard something had happened and wanted to see for themselves. "Perhaps we shouldn't try to get any closer."

"Good point," Tom agreed. "They don't need more people crowding the scene."

"So, there is a scene."

"Let's walk on a bit and then cross the street. I see a gap in the corner opposite the hotel."

Tom waited for the traffic to ease up and, giving her a light tug, he urged her on.

"Not so fast, my hat nearly flew off. Not that it would be such a great loss."

They reached the other side of the street and swung

toward the crowd. Looking up, Evie saw people looking out of their hotel windows while those with balconies stood outside.

Crossing the street had been a sensible idea. From their vantage point on the corner, they could now see several police officers trying to push back the onlookers.

Around them, people were quiet, almost as if the occasion called for silence. But then, she heard someone murmuring.

"It could be a protestor. There seem to be more of those every day. Someone complaining about something or other."

Evie saw a few heads bobbing up and down in agreement.

"Mob mentality," someone else muttered. "They think they own the streets."

Evie felt her heart thump against her chest. She grabbed Tom's arm. "Caro."

"She's fine," Tom assured her. "Edmonds is with her."

"Yes, but something might have happened to her."

Tom scanned the street. Evie could see him doing a thorough sweep, missing no one. Of course, Caro might be stuck somewhere, much as they were, waiting for the crowd to clear.

"There." Tom pointed across the street. "She's in the hotel. Standing on your balcony."

Evie's hold tightened on his arm. She narrowed her gaze and tried to focus. Finally, she saw Caro and

Edmonds leaning on the balcony railing, appearing to look down.

"She has a bird's-eye view and will no doubt be able to tell us everything," Tom said.

Feeling somewhat relieved to see Caro hadn't come to any harm, Evie resumed her vigil of the scene across the street. "The police are making some headway. People are finally beginning to move."

Moments later, an ambulance appeared as well as police reinforcements.

Tom nudged her. "I think we should move away. You don't want to see this."

"See what? You saw something."

He gave a small nod. "There's a body on the sidewalk just outside our hotel. Someone might have collapsed."

Or worse, Evie couldn't help thinking.

"It will probably be some time before we can return to the hotel." He stopped. "Then again, there is a side entrance. Let's see if we can gain access that way."

They crossed the street, their steps hurried to avoid the traffic. When they reached the safety of the opposite sidewalk, Evie looked up and saw Caro still leaning over the balcony looking down.

"I'm not sure I would be doing that," Evie murmured.

"What?"

"I've never seen a dead body and I'm sure I don't wish to see one any time soon. Yet, Caro doesn't seem to mind. She must have a stronger constitution than I give her credit for." Evie shook her head. Why had she assumed Caro was looking down at a dead body?

Tom pointed toward the side door of the hotel. "The concierge is standing outside."

He greeted them and promptly opened the door.

"I'll meet you upstairs," Tom said and lingered by the door with the obvious intention of finding out what he could from the concierge.

Evie encountered a stairwell. She placed her hand on the railing, stopped and changed her mind. Instead of taking the back stairs, she made her way to the hotel lobby where she found guests milling about, some standing by the windows watching the scene outside.

Hurrying up the main stairs, she went directly to her room where she found Caro still standing outside on the balcony.

"Caro, thank goodness you are all right."

"Milady." Caro signaled for her to join her out on the balcony.

"That's quite all right, Caro. I'll just stand inside. Do you know anything?" Just then, Evie noticed Edmonds leaning against the railing.

Her chauffeur turned and nodded a greeting. "Milady. I hope you don't mind me being here…"

"That's quite all right, Edmonds." She turned to Caro again. "Did you see anything?"

"Edmonds and I had a wonderful afternoon strolling along the beach but then I told him I needed to return so I could organize your clothing for this evening…"

That didn't surprise Evie. Despite this being her

vacation, Caro had insisted she needed to continue with her duties.

"Edmonds went up to his room because he didn't want to miss a single moment of the view. A short while later, I heard a banging on the door. It was Edmonds."

The chauffeur gave a nod as if to confirm Caro's story.

"While I was busy organizing your gown, he walked out onto his balcony and he saw..." Caro gasped.

"Oh, heavens," Evie exclaimed. "What did he see?"

Caro took a deep swallow. "He saw the body a second before it hit the ground."

"H-hit the g-ground? Are you saying the person fell?"

Caro gave a stiff nod.

CHAPTER 4

*H*earing a knock at the door Evie hurried to answer it. "Tom. Come in. You'll never believe what Caro just told me."

Tom entered and followed Evie to the window. While Evie remained inside the room, he had no qualms about stepping out onto the balcony and looking down.

"The ambulance has just taken her away," Caro said and heaved in a big breath. "And the police have covered up the sidewalk. Oh, it must have been horrible. Falling and crashing against the pavement." She covered her face with her hands and shook her head.

"Caro, I think you should move away from there now," Evie urged.

Caro gave a vigorous shake of her head. "My legs are quivering but I can't stop looking down."

Employing her firmest tone, Evie ordered Caro to return inside. "I will call for some tea. This is going to give you nightmares." She placed the call and then returned to the window. "So, did you find out anything?" she asked Tom.

"The concierge only knows what a waiter told him. The waiter had been serving someone seated by the window and looked out in time to see a woman falling."

"Does he know who it was?"

Tom gave a small nod. "No one had a close look at her but judging by her clothes and shoes, the waiter thinks she was a maid here at the hotel."

Heavens above.

"Perhaps you should both come away from that balcony," Evie urged. "It might not be safe."

Tom inspected the railing and shook his head. "It's sturdy. This hotel has been fully refurbished. I doubt the owner would take any risks."

"Please come back inside. You're both making me tremble with fear. I'm sure that balcony was not designed to hold two grown men."

Edmonds and Tom exchanged a look that spoke of resignation and stepped back inside.

"What do you think happened?" Caro asked.

"The concierge assumes she leaned out too far and fell," Tom said.

An accident. Evie tried to imagine the maid out on the balcony. What would compel her to lean over the railing? She could have been shaking dust off something and... maybe her hold loosened and...

"You're grimacing," Tom remarked.

"I'm trying to understand what happened." She turned to Caro. "Can you think of a reasonable excuse for the maid to be out on the balcony? I can only think of her shaking something to clean it."

Before Caro could answer, they heard a knock at the door. Tom opened the door to a waiter who brought in tea and sandwiches.

Evie got busy pouring everyone a cup of tea. Settling down on the chaise longue at the foot of her bed, she took a revitalizing sip.

"I stood on that balcony for quite some time, milady," Caro finally said. "I can't imagine anything that would make me lean over."

"Not even if you nearly dropped something? Something of value?" Evie shivered and only then remembered afternoons tended to cool down by the seaside.

"I doubt anything would be worth risking my life over." Caro rummaged through Evie's luggage, produced a wrap and placed it around Evie's shoulders.

"Yes, please keep that in mind," Evie said. "Nothing is more important than your life."

Another knock at the door had everyone stilling.

Evie set her cup down. "I suppose the police will want to speak with us."

Tom went to answer the door. Seeing who it was, he slipped out and eased the door closed behind him.

"More tea anyone?" Evie offered.

Edmonds set his cup down. "I... I should go, milady."

Evie had noticed he hadn't looked comfortable

being in her room. "Nonsense. I'm sure the police will want to interview all the guests. Wait here for a while."

"As you wish, milady."

Evie had the sudden urge to telephone Henrietta but the telephone in her room was only connected for room service purposes. Finishing her tea, she considered pouring herself another cup when Tom returned.

"My apologies, that was the concierge."

"I take it you encouraged him to bring you some news," Evie said.

Tom nodded. "All the staff are accounted for except one. May Fields worked this morning and then she had the afternoon free."

"She fell off the balcony while still wearing her maid's clothes," Caro said. "That means she never left."

"Did the concierge know from which balcony she fell?" Evie asked.

"The police need to verify this. As I said, May Fields had the afternoon free so they will have to try to find her."

"But you said all the other staff are accounted for."

Giving a nod, Tom helped himself to some tea. "In answer to your question, the concierge assumes it was the room above yours. The maid had been assigned to clean the rooms in that floor. All the rooms have the balcony windows left open during the day. He showed a policeman through to each room but the policeman asked him to remain outside when he inspected the room directly above yours, so the concierge didn't have the opportunity to see anything of significance."

And Evie assumed he wouldn't think of returning to the room, despite having the master keys...

"So she... presumably fell from the balcony in the room directly above mine."

They all turned toward the balcony and stared in silence.

Evie set her teacup down and hugged herself. "I suppose the police will get to us eventually."

"No, the concierge just informed me the police have already finished their investigation," Tom said.

"Pardon? So quickly," Evie exclaimed. "They're not going to talk to all the guests?"

"They don't see the need to," Tom said. "They've spoken with the staff working at the hotel. Apparently, the maid hadn't been in good spirits."

Jumping to the only conclusion possible, Evie's eyes widened. "Are you saying she jumped to her death on purpose?"

"The poor soul," Caro whispered. "She must have been so unhappy. But... how could she be unhappy working in a place such as this one?"

Death by suicide.

Evie couldn't begin to grasp the idea either. Even in her darkest moment, she had never considered doing away with herself.

"Tom, could you see what else you can find out about the young woman? Her family will surely be devastated..."

"I'll talk to the concierge again."

Caro got up. "I think I should like to spend some time alone, milady."

"Yes, of course." She hoped this wouldn't spoil Caro's trip. Edmonds excused himself too. Left alone with Tom, Evie said, "We might have to cheer Caro up. I should hate for her to return home without any fond memories of her vacation."

Tom went to stand by the window. A moment later, he said, "Will you be having dinner downstairs or would you like me to find somewhere else?"

It seemed strange to make plans. But life went on, Evie thought and had to force herself to reply, "In the dining room, I think. I don't really feel like venturing out tonight."

"In an hour?"

Evie nodded and watched him leave. She imagined everyone wished to be left alone with their thoughts.

Looking up at the ceiling, she wondered about the guests staying in the room above her. If they had been out and about all day, they would now return to learn the news…

How dreadful, she thought. Looking around her, she wondered how she would feel about staying in a room where someone had jumped to their death…

Evie had nearly finished dressing when Caro knocked on her door and entered.

"Edmonds and I have decided to go out for dinner. We both need to distract ourselves."

"Yes, I don't blame you. Poor Edmonds. How is he feeling?" Evie imagined he would be trying to rid himself of the image. After all, he'd seen the young woman falling.

"Oh, he will be fine enough in no time, I'm sure. Men can be strange. They present a brave front but they hide their true feelings. I'm going to get him to talk about it. I think it will do us both good." Caro shook her head. "I... I can't stop thinking about that poor girl."

"No, nor can I. It's taken me twice as long to dress because I kept stopping to gaze out of the window. There are so many thoughts whirling in my mind. Why did she end it all? What pushes someone to take such drastic measures?"

Caro gave a pensive nod. "My mother is fond of saying we need to find our joy. Even in the smallest things we do."

Like taking a walk along the promenade, Evie thought. Lifting her chin, she decided she would return to the pier the next day and make sure she enjoyed her walk. She might even wear her cherry hat again and taunt the seagulls.

Caro picked up a hairpin. "Let me work on your hair. I need to do something."

Evie brushed a curl away from her eye. "Oh, I thought I did a fine job... but I guess it can always do with an expert hand."

"I saw Tom walking down to the hotel restaurant. He looks quite dapper in his tuxedo." Caro sighed and, after a moment of silence, said, "Why would she do something so rash? She could have talked with some-one. She could have found help."

"I suppose we can all learn something from this. If anything ever troubles you, Caro, I want to know you'll feel comfortable coming to me."

"Of course, milady. As my mother is fond of saying, a problem shared, is a problem halved."

CHAPTER 5

*E*vie encountered a few guests as she made her way down to the dining room. Everyone appeared to be oblivious of the day's events or simply determined to put it all behind them. It just seemed strange to hear people laughing. While she didn't expect the guests to go into a state of mourning, it would not be entirely out of place to maintain a more subdued tone.

By the time she reached the bottom of the stairs, she had seen enough joyful expressions to realize not everyone considered the death of a mere maid worth that much attention. She didn't want to think it true, but she knew most of the guests who could afford to stay in the hotel would possibly consider the death of no consequence. They might even think of it as an inconvenience spoiling their experience at the hotel.

She found Tom in the lobby. Smiling, she approached him. "I thought you would be waiting for me in the dining room."

"I've just had a word with the concierge so I decided to wait for you here."

Tom gave her his arm and they made their way through to a room styled in the latest trends with an abundance of gold trimming, hints of aqua and a lot of ebony. A soft piano tune wafted from the bar. The gentlemen were all dressed in tuxedos and the ladies looked resplendent in their evening gowns.

"I asked for a table in the middle. That way, we can keep an eye on everyone and continue with our game."

"My goodness, Tom. You seem to have thought of everything. And here I was thinking we would try to take our minds off and talk about… Well, I had been hoping you would be able to come up with something."

Smiling, he drew out a chair for Evie and then settled down to peruse the menu. Quirking an eyebrow, he said, "For once, I will not require a translation. Most of the menu is in English."

Studying her own menu, Evie asked, "Did the concierge have something new to say?"

"I managed to get him to reveal the identity of the room occupants. Mr. George Prentiss and his… wife."

"Why did you hesitate?"

"Possibly because the concierge hesitated. When I asked him about it, he looked askance and shrugged. How would you interpret his reaction?"

Evie tapped her menu. "The woman staying with Mr. Prentiss is not his wife?"

"That's my guess too. I also asked him about the room above that one."

In case the maid had fallen from a higher floor? But

the police had already decided she had been in the room above Evie's... Did Tom harbor doubts? "That was smart thinking. Who is staying in that room?"

"Aha, well... We are actually familiar with them. Mr. Hector Addington and Mrs. Addington. Remember, we saw them at the tea room earlier today."

"I take it they were out and about for the entire afternoon."

"Well, we know Mr. and Mrs. Addington were enjoying afternoon tea."

"Oh, yes. The happy couple. He's a banker and she's... extremely happy." Evie glanced around the restaurant but she couldn't see them. Leaning forward, she murmured, "Can you see them?"

He gave a small nod. "They are sitting two tables away from us, behind you."

"How do they look?"

"Still happy."

"Are you sure? The lights are muted here."

"And yet I can see Mrs. Addington smiling brightly. Wait... now she is laughing."

If someone had jumped to their death from her balcony or anywhere near her room, Evie didn't think she would be laughing. The thought lingered in her mind as a waiter took their orders and another one brought them complimentary glasses of champagne.

"I must confess," she said, "I am slightly disgruntled by the police. You would think they'd want to speak with all the hotel guests. We can't assume the hotel manager was able to provide them with all the information they required to reach their conclusion about May Field's death."

Running his finger along the stem of the glass, Tom said, "The hotel manager would have tried to avoid disrupting the guests. I don't imagine he would be happy about attracting publicity. In fact, with such a new establishment, they would try to keep the news out of the spotlight."

Evie took a sip of her champagne. "That doesn't justify being neglectful. I really don't wish to think the police would treat this incident with less interest just because the victim happened to be a maid."

"Not everyone shares your sense of equal justice."

Glancing around her, Evie would have to agree. She knew many people who would not bat an eyelid at the loss and would prefer such a matter be dealt with the greatest expediency.

"Earlier, I decided to be more appreciative of the small things in life." Evie gave him a brisk smile. "Yes, such as walks along the pier. I talked about it with Caro and she agrees. Death makes one more grateful and aware of our blessings. So, I should now be able to sit and enjoy a splendid meal. Yet I am struggling."

"You don't know that for sure. The first course hasn't been served yet."

Evie held her glass of champagne and gestured with it. "This is vintage champagne. Either the manager is trying to impress me or he is doing all he can to pacify the guests."

The maître d' approached them, his manner befitting someone eager to please. "I hope everything is to your satisfaction, Lady Woodridge."

It didn't surprise Evie to be addressed by her title. The manager would have made sure to acquaint all his staff members with information about particular guests.

"Yes, thank you. Mr. Winchester and I are quite happy."

The maître d' nodded. Before he could move onto the next table, Evie gestured for him to draw closer. "I wonder if you might assist us with some information."

He hesitated but then nodded. "I'll do what I can, my lady."

"It's regarding the unfortunate incident that took place earlier on. We wish to express our condolences to the family."

"I'm afraid that will not be possible, my lady. Unfortunately, the young woman did not have any family."

So... The police had made a positive identification. They must have determined the maid had not left the hotel, after all. "None whatsoever?" Evie could barely hide her dismay. "Where did she live before coming to work here?"

The maître d' hesitated again.

Evie assumed it wouldn't be appropriate to release such personal details. "We would greatly appreciate any information you could give us."

Lowering his voice to a whisper, he said, "I believe she lived north of Worthing, in a village nearby called Findon."

"Is it far from here?"

"A short distance, my lady. I believe it is about four miles."

Not far at all, Evie thought and glanced at Tom. He would be only too happy to drive there. "Thank you. You have been very helpful."

A waiter brought their entrée dishes. Evie leaned forward to see what Tom had ordered. "That looks appetizing."

"It's a shrimp cocktail. And I see you ordered the oyster cocktail."

In the spirit of appreciating her blessings, Evie told herself to focus on enjoying her meal and to leave everything else until tomorrow.

"Are you going to tell me what that was all about?" Tom asked.

"My interest in your entrée? Whenever I order something I'm afraid of making the wrong choice and finding the other person's entrée more enticing."

Tom took his time chewing his food and savoring his champagne. Finally, he said, "I was referring to your curiosity about May Fields' family."

"Oh, I thought we might leave all that until tomorrow. These oysters are divine."

Tom sat back and watched her in silence.

"Fine. I thought we might drive out to Findon."

"What do you hope to find there?"

"May Fields lived there. I assume there are people who knew her. They're bound to hear about her... passing." Evie reached for her glass only to set it down again. "Actually, now that I think about it, we should call in at the police station tomorrow. If she doesn't have any family, who will take care of making the arrangements for her? It shouldn't take us too long and then we could drive out to Findon. I'm sure you'll enjoy that. I promise not to complain if you drive too fast."

"Four miles. I can barely contain my excitement. I'm sure this is what a pet feels like when they're allowed out to run around the yard."

"Are you suggesting I have been keeping you on a tight leash?"

Tom smiled. "I would never dare imply such a thing."

They both leaned back slightly to allow the waiter to clear the entrée dishes. Evie watched him set her main course in front of her. She hadn't put much thought into her meal but, thinking it looked delectable, she took a moment to admire her Lobster Salad. It didn't surprise her to see Tom had opted for a beef dish. Before the waiter could leave, Evie called for his attention. "I wonder if you might recognize one of the guests staying here and if you might point them out to us."

The waiter nodded. "I'll do my best, my lady."

Ah, clearly all the staff had been informed of her identity. "Mr. Prentiss and his wife. Are they dining here this evening?"

The waiter glanced around the restaurant and then gave her a discreet nod toward a table in the corner.

"Thank you."

"That was..." Tom smiled and shook his head, "quick work."

"If you glance over to your right, you will see the waiter pointed at the other couple we saw at the tea room this afternoon. The couple who didn't look entirely happy." Evie thought they would now have less reason to be happy.

When Tom glanced at Mr. Prentiss and his wife, she said, "Your tact is to be applauded. I barely noticed you looking away."

"They still look... morose," he said. "Yes, I think that's it. Not entirely happy about something."

"I agree." As she took a bite of her lobster, Evie wondered how they could find out more about the Prentiss couple. "Do you think your concierge friend could enlighten you about them?"

"At the rate I'm paying him for information, I think he will be only too happy to dig up the family tree for us."

CHAPTER 6

"*I* hope you slept well, Caro."

"I'm almost embarrassed to say I did, milady. After dinner, Edmonds and I made our way to the pier. They had a live band." Caro's eyes brightened. "We strolled along to the end of the pier and watched the stars twinkling in the sky. I found the music rather comforting."

"I'm glad to hear you made the best of it last night. I really do want you to enjoy yourself, Caro."

"Did you and Tom enjoy your meal last night?" Caro asked.

Evie smiled. "We certainly did. I expect he will have some more information for me this morning."

"Oh? Information about what, milady?"

"As it turns out, we encountered both couples who are occupying the rooms directly above mine." Evie pointed to the ceiling. "Mr. Prentiss and his wife are occupying that room and Mr. Addington and his wife are in the room above that one."

Caro brought out a light green dress and held it out for Evie's inspection.

"I think the blue one will suit better this morning."

Caro's eyebrows rose a notch. "Are you planning a special outing?"

"Yes, we are paying the local constabulary a visit. I need to know if someone is making arrangements for May Fields." Evie glanced at Caro. "She doesn't have any family."

"Oh. I see. Yes, that is so sad. Is there something I can do?"

Evie studied her reflection in the mirror. She looked slightly pale that morning. While she had slept well, she had stayed up until late thinking about the reasons May Fields had chosen to end it all, right here at the hotel. Had she been trying to send a message? If she had chosen to kill herself in her apartment or wherever she lived, someone might have eventually found her. What method would she have employed? Evie glanced at the window. The hotel might have been the only place where May Fields could gain access to a floor a good distance above the ground...

"Caro. I know I'm trying to encourage you to enjoy yourself, but do you think you could find some time to speak with the maids at the hotel? I'd like to know more about May Fields. Did she have any friends here? Where did she live? Was she truly unhappy?"

Caro gave a firm nod. "Consider it done."

"Please don't let it take up all of your time."

"I promise." Caro gave her a small smile. "And... Thank you for caring."

Evie thought it was the least she could do. "I might not say it often enough… If at all. However, you make a difference in my life."

Caro laughed. "Oh, I know that already. I'm sure you couldn't go a day without me. I meant, thank you for caring about the maid."

"Well, if not me, I'm sure someone else would have looked into it." Evie didn't want to say it, but it would be sad to think no one would mourn for May Fields. Evie tipped her head in thought. She planned on making arrangements. Why had she said she was looking into it? Looking into what?

Evie slipped into her dress and shoes. "I'll need a hat too, please. Preferably one without fruit. The seagulls here are quite ravenous."

Caro produced a straw bucket hat with a blue band to match the dress and a bunch of pretty daisies nestled on one side.

"Yes, that will do nicely. Thank you."

～

Evie found Tom standing beside the roadster outside the hotel.

"The Prentiss couple just strolled by," he said. "They didn't look any happier."

Evie looked down the street and thought she spotted them. While everyone around them walked with a light spring to their step, they appeared to be dragging their feet.

"It makes one wonder what they are doing here. I

can't help feeling there is something in the air, something that would make even the most miserable soul break into a smile." Evie remembered the story she had made up about the couple. "Maybe he's not the one who lied about his fortune. What if it's the other way around. He married her thinking she had inherited a fortune and now he has found out she doesn't have a penny to her name and neither does he. So they don't know how they are going to cover all the expenses they are incurring here at the hotel. Until they figure it out, they will continue to stay here." Evie scooped in a breath and smiled.

"You look rather pleased with yourself."

"I keep telling you, it's the sea air. I think I will recommend a trip to the seaside to Henrietta. Perhaps Brighton. Anyhow, did you find out anything from the concierge?"

Holding the passenger door open, Tom said, "Nothing new. But at least we know the Prentiss couple are staying in the room directly above you. That could be the reason why they are still looking dejected."

"Do you think the police will confirm whether or not May Fields fell from the Prentiss balcony?"

"There is only one way to find out. What am I saying? Of course they will tell us. You'll make sure they do." As he pulled into traffic, he said, "I have made inquiries about the road to Findon. We are likely to drive through some rather pretty country. As it turns out, we would have driven out that way to see the flint mines. They have an annual Findon sheep fair in September. We're too early for that, unfortunately."

Evie didn't hide her surprise. "You would have been interested in that?"

"It must be quite a sight." He nodded. "There's a church and you'll never guess. It's made of flint."

"You're right. I would never have guessed."

A few minutes later, he brought the motor car to a stop outside the police building.

They walked inside with a sense of purpose. As they approached the front desk, a constable looked up and greeted them.

While the constable's attention went straight to Tom, Evie spoke first, "We would like to inquire about a recently deceased person. Her name was May Fields."

The constable looked from Tom to Evie and back to Tom again.

"And what is your interest in the matter?"

"We are guests at the hotel where the young woman died," Evie said beginning to feel slightly annoyed because instead of looking at her, the constable only made eye contact with Tom.

"My apologies, I should have introduced myself. I am Lady Woodridge and this is Mr. Winchester."

"We don't normally give out information to the public."

"I'm sure you could make an exception," Evie said. "From what I understand, May Fields didn't have any family. I wish to know if someone is making arrangements for her."

"You're quite right. No family to speak of. No one has come forward." The constable cleared his throat.

"As for the matter of arrangements... The parish will take care of it all."

"What sort of arrangements?"

The constable now looked slightly uncomfortable. "The usual arrangements."

"I'm afraid you will have to spell it out for me," Evie said.

"There will be the usual arrangements befitting an indigent person."

A pauper's grave? But May Fields had worked... she hadn't been poor or needy... Just because she didn't have any family didn't mean she should be labeled as indigent.

Evie dug out a card from her purse. "I should like to be responsible for suitable arrangements." She handed the card over. "Now, if we could please speak with someone in charge of the investigation."

"There is no investigation, Lady Woodridge."

Evie lifted her chin. "I should then like to speak with your superior."

Out of the corner of her eye, Evie saw Tom smiling at the constable. She imagined him daring the constable to defy Evie.

Shaking his head, the constable withdrew into an office.

Evie smiled at Tom. "I think that went rather well, don't you?"

Tom smiled "If you consider browbeating a police constable as doing well, then yes, I agree."

"I did no such thing. In fact, I displayed the utmost courtesy. The same can't be said for the constable."

A man emerged from the office adjusting his tie. He greeted them and introduced himself as Detective Inspector Hopper.

"How may I help you?"

Evie explained about their interest in May Fields. "I must say, I was surprised when we were not interviewed."

"Do you feel you would have been able to provide vital information, Lady Woodridge?" the detective asked.

"Not necessarily, but there was no way for you to know that."

Tom cleared his throat. Evie took it as a warning to tone it down.

"I would hate to think the lack of interest in the case has anything to do with the young woman's profession."

"Is that so?" The detective brushed a hand across his chin.

"I employ many servants and if any of them were to come to any harm, I would like to think their case would be treated with the same interest as that of someone of greater consequence."

"I can assure you, my lady, if one of your servants committed a crime they would be thoroughly investigated."

Evie gave him a tight smile. "That is not what I meant."

Tom suffered a fit of coughing.

"I would take care of that cough, Mr. Winchester. It sounds quite serious. Now, if you will excuse me, I have other matters to attend to." Giving a firm nod, the detective withdrew and disappeared back inside his office.

"I think we should walk away now, Evie," Tom suggested.

"Yes, I agree. Who knows what else I might say to that man." When they reached the roadster, she turned and scowled at the police precinct. "I found him to be rude, patronizing and uncooperative. You'll be pleased to know I look forward to a speedy drive along the countryside. I would like to put as much distance between us as we can in as short a time as possible, please."

Tom smiled. "I'll be more than happy to oblige."

CHAPTER 7

"Y ou've been quiet for miles now," Tom said slowing down as they approached the village of Findon.

"My apologies. I've spent the time trying to diffuse my anger toward the detective." Evie smiled at him through clenched teeth.

"Thank goodness. I thought your silence might have had something to do with me driving too fast." He brought the car to a stop at the edge of the village and looked up ahead. "So what is the plan now?"

Evie shook her head. "Someone around here must have known May Fields. We could walk around." She barely drew in her next breath when she added, "How can the detective be sure May Fields jumped to her death?"

Tom walked around the roadster and opened the passenger door for Evie. "You've lost me. Have you spent the last four miles holding a discussion with yourself?"

"Yes. As far as the police are concerned, this is an open and shut case. May Fields had been unhappy so she jumped to her death. Does that make sense to you?"

"It's a senseless death, Evie. I don't know about you, but I'm still trying to understand it. That's human nature. We try to make sense of something we don't understand and are not likely to until we experience it ourselves."

Evie crossed her arms and huffed out a breath. "I didn't even know this woman and yet, I can't stop thinking about her death. I'm no stranger to losing someone and I understand what it's like to actually go through a stage of disbelief, of not wanting to accept reality." She stared into the distance but didn't focus on anything in particular. "What if... What if the police are dismissing this death when they should actually be looking into it? Yesterday, we were playing a game, inventing stories about people. On the surface, we can look so normal and quite harmless, but we could be harboring the darkest secrets, secrets no one could possibly imagine." She shook her head. "Never mind. Let's walk on. I think I see a sign up ahead. It might be a tea room."

"Yes, I wouldn't mind stopping for a cup of something."

"I thought we might ask in there about May Fields."

"Of course. But... We could still have something to drink."

Evie glanced at Tom. "You're worried about me."

He slipped his hands inside his pockets and

shrugged. "Well, you do seem to be taking this unfortunate incident hard."

"Either that, or I'm making the best of a dreadful situation. The more I think about it, the more I believe there might be something more to her death… Since I can't shake the feeling away, we could continue on with our game. I don't see any harm in it and it might help me to move on…"

"Yes, I suppose we could do that. Although, other than coming to terms with it, I'm not sure what else you hope to achieve."

Evie turned her attention to walking and making sure she didn't stub her toe on the cobblestones or miss her step and twist her ankle. "I just think…" She pushed out a breath. "I just think the police should have put more effort into the investigation. It all happened so quickly. How do they know they haven't missed something crucial? Once they removed the body, it was all over. I think I managed to drink two cups of tea when you came in and told us the police had already decided May Fields had jumped to her death."

"Would you be happier if the police had interviewed you?"

"I don't know." She couldn't really say with any degree of certainty. The police might have spoken with her and still reached the same conclusion about May Fields' death because, of course, she would not have been able to contribute any insightful information, and, yes… She would still wonder.

Had the young woman jumped to her death? Or…

What if someone had pushed her?

She played around with that idea. Motive. Yes, the police always looked for motive. Jealousy? Resentment? May Fields might have had an enemy. One of the other maids? A waiter? The manager? The concierge?

She knew the police also looked at opportunity. That is, when the police actually decided to investigate an incident.

May Fields had been cleaning a room. If someone had caught her by surprised, they might have overpowered her and pushed her off the balcony. Surely, there would have been a struggle, in which case, the police would have seen proof of it.

Clearly, they hadn't seen anything to trigger their suspicions.

"Forget I said anything."

They walked in silence, admiring the pretty cottages with their colorful blooms and lace curtains billowing in the light breeze.

"It must be dreadfully inconvenient to live so close to the road," Evie remarked. "If you had come roaring through this street, you might have given someone an attack." Some of the cottages had windows right on the edge of the property next to the street. In fact, some were so close she could peer inside.

"With more and more people owning motor cars these day, someone will eventually need to rethink this road system," Tom mused.

"What do you suggest they might do?"

He looked around. "Build a road nearby, circumventing the village with this road here connecting to it further ahead. Eventually, someone will realize the traffic will increase and, as you have noted, the houses are close to the road. It will become an inconvenience."

"You said there's a church here."

Tom nodded.

"I'm guessing it was built a couple of hundred years ago. Back then, no one really thought about motor cars taking over. Oh…"

"What?"

"I'm not sure I should tell you."

"Is this because I'm not entirely onboard with your growing suspicions about May Fields' death? Or rather, your dissatisfaction with the brief police investigation?"

"Maybe." Evie shrugged. "Fine. If no one here knows May Fields, we could go to the church. They are bound to have records of everyone born in the area."

"That's actually a very good idea." Tom pointed ahead. "There's that sign you saw. You're right. It looks like a tea room."

Drawing closer, they saw a couple emerging and walking in the opposite direction.

"I guess this is as good a time as any for tea."

They walked in and found a quaint establishment with small round tables. Two ladies sat in a corner table. They looked up, smiled and then resumed their conversation.

A young woman approached them. "Table for two?"

Evie nodded and they were shown to a table by the window. As they sat down, a motor car drove by. The windows rattled slightly and then settled.

"I suppose you would get used to it," Evie murmured.

After a brief glance at the menu they ordered some tea and scones with clotted cream and strawberry jam.

The young woman set the tea cups and plates down. When she brought the tea, Evie asked if she knew May Fields.

"Yes, indeed." Her cheeks colored slightly. "We heard the dreadful news."

So quickly?

"One of the locals travels down to Worthing every day to work. Word spread last night. We are all in shock."

"Did you know her personally?"

"Oh, no... Not really. She is... was a couple of years older than me. She used to work here before she decided she wanted something better. From what I hear, May Fields always wanted something better. I don't mean that in a bad way."

"Of course, you don't." Evie gave her a warm smile. "Did she live nearby?"

The waitress nodded. "She used to work for Mrs. Daulton up the street as a live-in maid. Then she came to work here."

"Do you know if she had any close friends?"

"Ruth Charles. They were always seen chatting together..."

Evie didn't need to ask where she might find Ruth Charles because the young woman happily supplied the information.

A couple entered the tea room and the waitress excused herself.

"Well, now we have our afternoon mapped out for us," Evie declared.

"What do you hope to find?" Tom asked.

"I'm hoping to learn something about May Fields. We already know she wanted something better. Does that sound like someone who would kill herself?"

"No, indeed, it doesn't. But, we don't know what happened between here and her time working in Worthing."

"Precisely. Did something or someone snuff out her dreams? She might have had a bad experience with someone…" Evie poured the tea and turned her attention to spreading some jam on her scone. Looking up, she saw Tom looking at her. "I'm not going to justify my curiosity. And, it's not part of a game. I am truly concerned about the police spending so little time investigating her case. I can't help feeling they only skimmed the surface and tried to get through it all as quickly as possible." She knew it would have been a different story if one of the guests had fallen off the balcony…

Tom lifted his cup only to set it down. "All I can say is that the police usually work with physical evidence. If they had perceived some sort of foul play, something out of place, I am sure they would have followed up on it."

"What you are really saying is that if I feel the way I do, I should have some sort of solid proof or some sort of lead."

Tom sat back, his tea forgotten. "Until now, I assumed you were annoyed with the police because they appeared to have dismissed the death with a blitheness that suggested they simply didn't care… because May Fields was only a maid. Are you now saying you have a strong feeling about this?"

Evie gave it some thought. "The police won't take action unless they have reason to do so. Fine. Let's find a reason. Let me rephrase that. Let's ask some questions, learn as much as we can about May Fields and see where that leads us. I need to satisfy my curiosity."

Tom sat back and drank his tea. When he finished, he said, "How do you propose to do that?"

"We have already started by coming here. We'll talk to her friend and hopefully she might be able to tell us something else about May Fields. And we'll continue until someone says something of interest."

He raised an eyebrow as if surprised. "This really isn't a game for you now."

"No, but there's no reason why we couldn't see it as such. Our little game didn't really have any rules and I think that rather helps. It gives us some leeway to use our imagination. For instance, when we talked about Mr. Addington, you said he was a banker. We all have very fixed perceptions of bankers. They are trustworthy, or at least we hope so. They are also serious. Personally, I think someone who spends a great deal of time with numbers is a little dull." Evie looked down and smiled. "I only say that because I am hopeless with numbers. Anyhow, I didn't have any compunction about labeling him a rebel, going against his family wishes and marrying someone his family had disapproved of. I'm willing to bet anything my description of him is spot on." She gave a small nod and added, "Despite all appearances. The same reasoning can be applied to May Fields' death. On the surface, it looks like an accidental death. What if it's not? By meeting people acquainted with May Fields, we might perceive something that might have provided someone with an ulterior motive to kill her."

"And what have you learned so far?"

Evie glanced at the waitress. "May Fields had dreams and she aspired to something better. That's why she moved to Worthing. We've already established that. I hope her friend, Ruth Charles, will reveal more about May's dreams. Think about it. With enough people telling us May Fields wanted more, we can create a picture of her character. I can already see it taking shape and it is leading me to believe she was not the type of person to give up and kill herself."

Tom poured himself another cup of tea. "Yes, fine. I see your point. However, if you do find something to justify your suspicions, it will have to be solid proof. Otherwise, I fear, the police will not take you seriously." He helped himself to a scone and a generous helping of clotted cream and strawberry jam.

Evie smiled. "I'm glad you put up some opposition. I would hate to think you would simply agree with me."

"It must have something to do with being let off my leash and allowed to drive fast. Now I'm reveling in my newfound freedom."

CHAPTER 8

"That looks like the house. The waitress said to look out for an abundance of yellow roses." Evie curled her toes inside her shoes. They had walked to the end of the main road but hadn't seen any yellow roses so they had doubled back and turned into another street. "By the way, yesterday you mentioned finally settling down when you found an article of interest but you didn't mention anything about what the article was about."

Tom looked away and cleared his throat.

"You don't want to discuss it?"

"I had been trying to steer you away from thinking about the maid falling off the balcony."

"So, you made up a story about finding an article of interest?"

"No, I did find something… Fine, it was an article about a murder suspect being apprehended."

"Oh, I see. You have been fixating on murder."

"I see someone coming out of the house," Tom said.

A young woman carrying a basket. She stopped for a moment to fix her hat and look inside her basket. While Evie didn't want to jump to conclusions, she thought it would be safe to assume the young woman worked as a servant in the house.

When Evie called out her name, the young woman hesitated, but Evie didn't see anything odd about that. Her cheeks also colored slightly and she looked at Evie and Tom with a hint of wariness. Again, Evie didn't find her behavior odd. After all, they were strangers in the village.

Evie introduced herself and confirmed the young woman's identity. When she told Ruth Charles she was staying at the hotel where May Fields had worked as a maid, the young woman took a deep swallow.

"I am very sorry for your loss," Evie said.

Ruth Charles looked down and shook her head. "I couldn't believe it at first. I still don't. I had planned to visit at Christmas time. We... We made plans and I was going to bake her favorite plum pudding as a gift."

"You were close."

Ruth kept her eyes lowered. "We both grew up in the same village nearby."

"And when she went to work in Worthing, you kept in touch."

Ruth nodded. "She wrote whenever she could and always encouraged me to leave here and seek a position at Worthing or Brighton. But I like it here. That's where we were different. Although, sometimes I thought about it. I think I will still think about finding another position. Maybe not so much now that this has happened."

"Did she ever mention someone she might have met at Worthing?"

Ruth hesitated and then gave a brisk shake of her head. "No, No one. She always wrote about the different people staying at the hotel and went on about the ladies' gowns and how posh the place was. May always liked nice things and on her half days off, she'd always wear her prettiest dress and pretend to be a grand lady. She said she used to take afternoon tea at one of the tea rooms and hold conversations with herself, always pretending she was one of the ladies. It was all fun and games to her. She told me she went to see a play once and had loved it so much, she dreamed of being a stage actress."

"So, she wanted to improve her life."

Ruth's cheeks colored. She gave Evie a brisk smile. "S-she liked to daydream but she was happy working as a maid because it gave her the time to dream." Ruth hesitated, then hurried to add, "When she worked here at the tea room, the proprietress had wanted to train her to do the books because she was smart with numbers but May lost interest. She said doing the books made her think too hard and she didn't have time to daydream." Ruth gave a sorrowful shake of her head. "Now she won't dream no more... I mean, any more."

"When did you last hear from her?" Evie asked.

Ruth met her gaze. Giving a tentative nod, she said, "A month ago." She dug inside her bag and produced a folded piece of paper. "This is the letter she wrote. See, here's the date." Looking over her shoulder, she excused herself saying she needed to run an errand.

"Well," Tom said, "what do you make of that? Oh, wait. Let me guess. She lied through her teeth."

"Mr. Tom Winchester, have some pity for that poor girl. Couldn't you see she was grieving?"

"Actually, no. Shouldn't her eyes be puffy or... her cheeks blotchy from crying? She just lost her best friend."

"Not everyone wears their heart on their sleeve," Evie said.

"So, you believed everything she said."

"I have no reason to doubt her." In the first days after losing her husband, Evie had sounded like a somnambulist, her words coming out in complete sentences but without any real spark or enthusiasm. Anyone might have thought she had been unfeeling. In reality, she had been hollow inside.

"Where do we go from here?" Tom asked.

"We could walk around and hope someone else can tell us more about May Fields but it might look odd if we stop everyone we encounter and ask questions." Evie looked around. "Besides, there don't appear to be many people out and about. It would definitely look awkward if we start knocking on doors. Perhaps we should head back."

"As long as we're here, we might as well have a look at the flint mine..."

Heavens. Evie had hoped he'd forgotten about the flint mine...

~

"In my defense, if we hadn't gone to see the flint mine, I would not have known there really wasn't much to see and I would have felt I'd missed out on something."

Evie patted Tom on the shoulder. "I didn't say anything, Tom."

"You were thinking it. In fact, I'm sure you were thinking something along the lines of so much for the flint mine."

Evie laughed. "I don't blame you, I'm sure you expected more. I suppose it's interesting enough to know ancient people mined it. In fact, if you think about it, we stood right where someone stood hundreds of years ago." Evie tilted her head. "Then again, we do that practically every day of our lives."

"You're amusing yourself at my expense." Tom drummed his fingers on the steering wheel. "I didn't know enough about the flint mines to actually appreciate what I was looking at. I'm sure an expert would be able to point that out to me."

"Would you like to find an expert?"

Tom murmured something she didn't quite understand under his breath.

Clearing his throat, he said, "Lunch. We could return to the hotel or stop somewhere as soon as we reach Worthing. Which will happen at any moment now."

"Lunch sounds like a good idea." Evie looked down at herself. "Although, I'm not really dressed for it."

"In other words, you would like to return to the hotel to change."

"Now that you mention it, yes. That would be lovely. Thank you for suggesting it. You might want to change out of those dusty clothes too."

"Now that you mention it... I have no choice."

Being driven along the main street that ran alongside the beach gave Evie the opportunity to watch everyone going about their business as if nothing had happened. In time, she thought, everyone would have forgotten about the incident outside the St. James Hotel.

Tom brought the roadster to a stop right in front of the hotel so they didn't have far to walk.

As Evie stepped out of the roadster, she stopped and gazed down at the sidewalk. The hotel staff had done a thorough job of cleaning up. She couldn't see any sign of the distressing incident from the day before.

"I know we didn't talk about this. I suppose there would have been a lot of damage to her body."

Tom lowered his voice. "She fell face down. I imagine all the bones would have been shattered."

The sun broke through the clouds. Yet, Evie shivered and hurried inside the hotel. "I'll see you shortly."

She let herself into her room, took off her hat and sat on the edge of the chaise longue at the foot of her bed. Had the trip to Findon been worth their while? It didn't feel like it.

She hoped Caro had made some progress with the maids. They had told the police May Fields hadn't been happy. Had they noticed anything else about her?

Evie sat back. May's friend, Ruth Charles, had said she'd been a dreamer. She'd received a letter from her only a month before. They'd made plans for Christmas.

What had happened during the last few weeks to change her life? What had made her unhappy?

Evie remembered mentioning the possibility of May Fields having an encounter with someone but she hadn't discussed it at great length with Tom. What if one of the hotel guests had accosted her and made an improper advance?

The experience might have been too much for a young woman from a small village... May Fields might have felt ashamed and unable to confide in anyone. She would have carried that burden. Yes, she might even have felt ashamed. That could definitely change the way a person felt about life.

Evie tipped her head back and stared up at the ceiling. Just then, the door to her room opened and Caro came in.

"Milady! I came in on the off chance that you might be here."

"Oh, Caro. I hope you've had some luck."

Caro got busy selecting a gown for Evie. "I spoke with all the maids."

"All of them!"

Caro nodded. "I started on this floor and made my way up. I found everyone I met quite lovely. For some reason, I had assumed they wouldn't all be nice. I only have experience working in a large house and we tend

73

to be a bit uppity about our roles." Caro laughed. "Some of us think we're better off working for a prominent family because it feels more prestigious. Personally, I like the feeling of belonging, of walking into the kitchen and knowing everyone. Of course, I'm sure that happens here too... Anyway, I'm prattling on. They all said the same thing about May Fields. She worked hard and never slacked off. Also, she never missed a day of work."

"Did anyone mention anything about her being unhappy?"

"One maid said May had been quiet the last few days and not her usual cheerful self."

"What about friends?"

"No. One maid said she'd invited her to go to a fair but May liked to take her half days in the middle of the week and go out alone."

Evie remembered Ruth saying May Fields enjoyed playing at make-believe.

Evie looked down at her hands. "Did she have any special friendships with the men working here?"

"I thought you might want to know about that so I asked and, no, she didn't. I had already spoken with the waiters and they all sounded lovely but I wanted to find out how the maids felt about them."

"What made you think to ask?"

Caro blushed slightly. "Well, Edmonds and I have been talking and we are having trouble believing she jumped to her death..."

Evie's lips parted. Had she found allies in Edmonds and Caro? She hadn't been able to convince Tom of her rising suspicions. Then again, she suspected he might be helping her in other ways. With good reason, Evie thought. The police had already shown a lack of interest in the case. If she wanted them to look into it further, she would have to present a strong case. Tom, whether he realized it or not, had been giving her a gentle encouragement. The moment she knew she had convinced Tom, she would know she had solid proof to present to the police.

Caro continued by saying, "I've heard of a few incidents where a footman got a bit fresh with one of the maids. It's possible the same thing happened here and May couldn't deal with it."

"Did any of the maids at the hotel express concerns about the guests?"

Caro looked pleased with herself when she said, "I asked about that too. They have a strict no-nonsense policy here and anything out of order has to be reported to the manager."

"Well, I'm glad to hear someone is doing right by the staff here." Evie looked toward the window. "What else did you discuss with Edmonds?"

"We were only wondering if she might've had a reason to jump."

What if May Fields had given someone a reason to push her?

CHAPTER 9

"The hotel manager runs a tight ship," Evie said as she settled down to lunch with Tom. "He doesn't allow any shenanigans to take place at his hotel."

"Is that what he would like everyone to believe?" Tom asked.

Evie sat back and studied him. "You are taking your devil's advocate duties so seriously, I'm having trouble deciding who's side you are on."

"I'm on your side, Countess."

When had Tom Winchester started calling her Countess? And what did it mean?

It had taken some doing but she had finally managed to convince him to stop using her title. He had then moved on to calling her ma'am. Even with his Boston accent, it had sounded too formal so Evie had pushed to convince him to use her first name, something even Henrietta, a stalwart observer of etiquette, found quaint. Although, the dowager still believed Tom

Winchester was a friend from back home. Regardless, even if Henrietta knew Tom was Evie's bodyguard, she would still find it all quaint and amusing.

Evie drummed her fingers on the table. He'd referred to her as Countess once before. This would be the second time. Evie decided to wait longer before forming any opinions.

Looking over his shoulder, she said, "Mr. and Mrs. Prentiss have taken a table behind you." Lowering her voice, she added, "They still look somber. There is definitely something wrong with that couple. They should be ecstatically happy to be here, enjoying their stay."

"Are they directly behind me?" Tom asked.

"Two tables away, but sound travels. I suggest referring to them as the quietly morose couple."

"Have you become suspicious of them?" Tom asked.

Yes, but only after talking with Caro. What if someone had pushed May Fields? "It makes sense to start looking at motives and suspects. You say the police look at the physical evidence. Clearly, they did not find any. Or... they didn't look hard enough."

"It's possible the police know something you don't and see no reason to pursue the matter," Tom reasoned.

"Are you suggesting they might have known about some sort of mental affliction which led her to end her life? That's not possible. All the maids say she was a happy sort." Evie took a sip of water and told herself Tom had every right to hold his own opinions. "Where was I?"

"You were telling me about your suspicions."

"Oh, yes... We know May Fields cleaned the room

above mine and we also know the quietly morose couple is currently staying there."

"And?"

"I have always been slightly wary of quiet people. What aren't they saying? What are they hiding? More to the point. What is he hiding?"

Tom employed his utmost discretion to look around. A moment later, he straightened. "Are you about to suggest he behaved in an unacceptable manner?"

Leaning forward, she murmured, "Actually, I had been playing around with the idea of him being the type who always misbehaves because he knows he can get away with it by issuing threats." She drew in a breath and delivered her character portrait. "He always makes sure to pick someone who is his social inferior and, perhaps, dependent on him for their livelihood. He is a devil in disguise and he uses a façade of unhappiness to hide the character trait. Anyone who knows him would describe him as an amiable man. Polite, quiet and an upstanding member of his community."

"You have a vivid imagination, Countess."

There it was again! "Yes, but do you approve of my theory?" She hoped she wouldn't have to spell it out to him.

"I wouldn't discount it." Tom looked around again. "I will have to have a word with the concierge. He might impart some information about the couple."

"Caro did splendidly today. I only asked her to have a chat with the maids and she ended up asking quite a few pertinent questions. Some of which hadn't even occurred to me. But it was all enough to set my mind alight with ideas." Perusing the menu, Evie wondered if she could get away with ordering some sandwiches because she would prefer to focus all her attention on finding a solid lead. Without one, May Fields might never get justice. "What are you ordering?"

"Fillet Mignon with potatoes. I believe I will need some sustenance to keep me going. Or, rather, to help me keep up with you."

"I think I'll have the same."

"Tell me more about your theory. What do you think happened here?"

"As unpalatable and disturbing as it might sound, he might have used her." Evie cringed at the thought of him forcing himself on the poor woman. In the next instant, Evie changed her mind. "Perhaps not in the way I originally thought." Evie gazed into the distance. "Now I'm thinking he might have made promises he had no intention of keeping. This is the scenario. May Fields is a dreamer. She dreams of a better life. He offers her that. Once he has his way with her, he shatters her dreams by dismissing her. Broken-hearted, she decides she cannot live without him so she ends it all."

Tom's eyebrows curved up. "You think he is a scoundrel who sold her a few empty promises." He brushed his hand across his chin. "I'm having trouble seeing May Fields as a gullible victim. I believe if she had felt duped, she would have taken matters into her own hands."

Evie closed her eyes for a moment. She hadn't actually drawn a picture of May. In fact, she had no idea what she had looked like. Making a mental note to ask Caro if she could ask around, she said, "Yes, you're right. So, let's follow that line of thinking. She's angry because he promised her a better life so she threatens to tell his wife. Worse. She knows he is a lawyer so she will contact his legal firm and tell them what he has done. She will move heaven and earth to discredit him and bring his real character to light."

Tom leaned forward, his eyes fixed on Evie's. "And he decides to stop her."

Evie's eyes widened in surprise. "Yes."

Lowering his voice, Tom said, "By pushing her off the balcony."

Oh, well… Yes. But when? They had seen the couple at the tea room. "I'm guessing you now wish to know when he might have carried out his nefarious act. I'm going to ask for some leeway. We'll continue working on my theory and then iron out the details."

"You wish to work with broad brushstrokes and then add in the details."

"Tom, I had no idea you had an interest in painting."

"I'm sure I read the reference somewhere."

Their meals were served, and Evie suddenly found her appetite.

"We need to find out if this is the first time Mr. P has stayed in this hotel. Oh… what am I saying. Of course, it is. The hotel has only recently opened. I wonder…" How could they look into his life? Did she know someone she could contact? Yes! Evie brightened. She could telephone her man of business in town… "I aim to find out everything I can about him.

Where he works, where he lives. Which club he belongs to."

Tom studied her for a long moment before saying, "You want to launch an investigation into the morose couple?"

"She fell to her death in their room. It makes sense to turn our focus on him."

Evie glanced toward the couple in question. Did the wife know about her husband's philandering activities? Some women were prepared to turn a blind eye to their husband's questionable behavior for the sake of avoiding a scandal. "We should at least find out if they are newlyweds." Giving a firm nod, she added, "I'll contact my man of business. He might be able to dig up some information."

Tom smiled. "I believe you are about to establish a network of spies. You already have Caro trained to ask questions you haven't even considered."

"Yes, and you are playing a pivotal role too. I have decided to welcome your opposition. You can make sure I don't make a fool of myself." Evie played around with her meal. "Do you think Detective Inspector O'Neill would welcome a telephone call from me?"

"There is only one way to find out."

A while later, Evie stirred her coffee and tried to remember what she usually talked about during a meal when another thought intruded. "I wonder if we could have a look inside Mr. Prentiss' room."

"What happened to contacting Detective Inspector O'Neill?"

"We will do that as soon as I figure out how to contact him. I have his telephone number."

"So, what's the delay?"

Evie glanced around and lowered her voice. "Privacy. I suppose we could ask the manager to use his office."

"If you are afraid of being overheard, I could stand outside and make sure no one goes near the door."

Evie thought about it and then shook her head. "I might need your help with the detective. Yes, I have been helpful in the past but even I am willing to admit I have nothing but flimsy suspicions and they're mostly based on the local constabulary not being thorough." Evie brightened. "He might listen to you. Also, men have a way of communicating with each other with few words. If I prattle on and confuse him, you can have a word with him and he'll be so relieved, he'll agree to anything."

"I'm glad to know I can be of some service."

"Tom, I hope you are not feeling superfluous. Without your valuable assistance, I would never have dreamed of delving into any of the incidents we have been involved in." She held up a finger as if she'd suddenly been struck by an idea. "I know. Caro can help us. She can find out when the maid goes into the room to clean and we can sneak in." Seeing Tom's look of confusion, she added. "Remember, earlier I mentioned wanting to see inside Mr. Prentiss' room."

"And, in the process, get the maid fired."

"Nonsense. If we are caught, I will simply play my Countess card."

"Remind me again about that card."

"Oh, I'll be all snooty, demanding and offended." She finished her coffee and smiled. "Now, let's see if the manager will allow us to use his office." When they walked out into the lobby, Evie hesitated.

"Is something wrong?" Tom asked.

"No, not really. Only… After that lunch I think a walk along the pier might do me a world of good. Perhaps after we've made the telephone call."

Mr. Richard Henderson, the hotel manager, responded to Evie's request with the swiftness of someone eager to please. Or, at least, appear to want to please.

Evie thought she detected a slight hardness in his eyes. Then she remembered going over his head to sort out her hotel reservations and finally getting her way. He could not have been pleased about that.

"Right this way, my lady."

Evie made sure to give him her warmest smile. "Thank you. It's very kind of you."

Evie entered the office and took in the large desk and high-backed leather chair. She thought she could smell a hint of cigar and imagined Mr. Richard Henderson making himself quite comfortable behind closed doors.

Searching through her handbag, she drew out a

small leather-bound notebook and found Detective Inspector O'Neill's contact number.

It took a moment to be connected, during which time, she stared at Tom.

He stood by the door as if standing guard but when Evie signaled with a nod, he approached the desk and sat down opposite her.

"Detective Inspector O'Neill. It's Evie." She had considered using her full name but thought a more casual approach might make him more amenable to assisting her with her investigation.

"Lady Woodridge, how wonderful it is to hear from you."

"Detective, I know your time is valuable so I will cut straight to the chase. There has been an incident at the hotel where we are currently staying." Evie proceeded to provide the detective with the story about the maid falling from the balcony to her death.

When she explained her displeasure at the lack of interest from the police, the detective fell silent.

"I realize you might not appreciate hearing such news about a colleague and I am sorry but I cannot help it. I find they were too dismissive of the situation."

"What exactly do you wish me to do?" The detective cleared his throat. "That is, assuming I am prepared to do anything."

Evie shifted to the edge of the chair. "Well, I should like to know more about Mr. Prentiss. He is a lawyer and I assume he works in town. I wonder if he has ever come under scrutiny for... something." She didn't want to go into what that something might have been.

If she was right about his character, Mr. Prentiss might be the type of man who made a habit of accosting vulnerable young women. One of his victims might have made a complaint to the police. Evie explained this, adding, "There might not be a record of the complaint. At least, not a public record but someone might know something..."

CHAPTER 10

"What else did the detective say?" Tom asked when they reached the end of the pier.

Evie had suggested taking a walk so they wouldn't have to worry about being overheard. Mostly, she had needed a breath of fresh air to clear her head and recover from the surprise. The detective had actually been quite helpful.

"Who was the last person to see May Fields alive? In other words, he suggested following police procedures and retracing the victim's steps." When Tom quirked his eyebrows up, she said, "I know, I am as surprised as you are. However, he did spend a great deal of time trying to dissuade me from taking an interest. Actually, while he employed those words, I'm sure he meant to say I should not meddle in police business. That's when I told him someone had to champion the poor girl's cause."

"I think I can well imagine his reaction to that."

Evie smiled. "Can you? Oh, do share your male insights."

"The detective would have sighed. He might have loosened his tie and brushed his hand across his brow. He might also have checked the time or signaled to someone and whispered for assistance. I'm thinking he might have tried to get someone to call him away on serious police business."

Evie's eyes widened. "You think he did all that? I'm going to have to trust your insightful knowledge because I can only picture him sitting back, open mouthed with disbelief and awe and maybe even a hint of appreciation and admiration."

Tom laughed.

"Anyhow, when I slipped upstairs to change into my walking clothes, I met Caro and asked her to make a few inquiries about May Fields' activities during her last day. I am willing to bet anything, by the time we return, she will have found out all we want to know about May Fields' last few hours."

Evie felt quite pleased with her efforts. Her conversation with the detective had been followed with a brief telephone call to her man of business in town. "I think we should have some answers from Mr. Matthew Keys sooner than we imagine possible. I trust my man of business implicitly. When I next speak with him, he will have found out everything there is to know about Mr. Prentiss Esquire."

"Shall we take another turn around the pier?"

"Yes. I still need to find out why Caro finds it so delightful." Evie turned and looked back toward the rows of elegant buildings facing the ocean. "There is something wonderfully understated about this resort town. Back home, this might all have been turned into an elite site for the very wealthy to parade their wealth to other people in the same social set."

"Yes, I wonder how that happens."

"The very rich like to stick together. Some might say they herd in colonies. I've heard of wealthy people choosing a place and clustering other top-drawer people around them. Oh, and the houses they build can be... Well, words fail to describe what some of those houses look like."

"Ostentatious?" Tom suggested. "Tawdry? Garish? Gaudy?"

"Oh, yes. I sometimes forget you are well-acquainted with some of the retreat towns back home." When Evie had told her granny she planned on returning to England, Toodles had insisted she needed a new chauffeur, who had turned out to be a body-guard in disguise. Tom had come to work for her months before her trip so they had both traveled around quite a bit.

"However, some of the houses are superb," Evie continued. "Granny mentioned a new one cropping up in an out-of-town retreat north of Philadelphia. I believe the owner has already named it. Let me think... Oh, yes. *Whitemarsh Hall.* Everyone is talking about it. They are intrigued by the fact it will have 147 rooms. Granny expressed surprise at such an extravagant investment. It is well known the owner is definitely not top-drawer."

"I'm sure he will throw the most lavish affairs at this new monument to wealth and all your pals will attend, even if in private they will sneer at the presumptuousness."

Evie smiled at Tom's mocking tone. "Yes, and I'm sure in time his humble beginnings will all be forgotten. Heavens, even the Vanderbilts had humble beginnings."

When they found themselves at the end of the pier again, Evie glanced around. "No. I am none the wiser. But if Caro finds this pier delightful, then that is good enough for me. Shall we head back?"

"My lady, there is a message for you." Bowing his head slightly, the concierge handed Evie a folded piece of paper.

Evie stepped away from the front desk and read the missive. "It's from the detective. He wants me to telephone him." Evie put away the note. "We shall have to impose on the manager again."

Tom took care of it. Moments later, Evie sat in the manager's office. When her call was connected, she greeted the detective with surprise. "What have you discovered and, might I add, so quickly."

"Nothing good, I'm afraid, my lady. I spoke with my colleague in Worthing." The detective cleared his throat. "Actually, would it be possible to speak with Mr. Winchester?"

Realizing the detective might want to tackle a delicate matter, she agreed. "One moment, please." Looking up at Tom, she said, "The detective wishes to speak with you."

She tried to read Tom's expression as he listened to the detective but the man knew how to keep his expression blank.

Biding her time, Evie glanced around the manager's office. He kept a tidy desk. The ink blotter only had a few ink stains on it and she imagined he had it changed on a regular basis. There were two framed photographs on his desk. One of a young woman and the other of an elderly woman. She guessed one might be his wife and the other his mother. Since she hadn't noticed a wedding band on his finger, she changed her mind and decided the young woman had to be his sister.

"I certainly will, detective." Tom disconnected the call. "The detective sends his regards."

"Oh, how very gracious of him." Evie waited for Tom to relate the details of their conversation and hoped she wouldn't need to prompt him.

"I think we might need to take another walk," Tom said.

"Are you about to impart bad news?"

"You might not like what I have to say."

"In that case, I might need to retire to my room and order a bottle of whiskey."

Giving a small nod, Tom said, "The detective spoke with his colleague. To quote Detective Inspector O'Neill, the Worthing detective took your female sensitivities into account. There is one piece of information he failed to reveal because of that."

"Tom, I am about to have a huffing fit. Please tell me."

"May Fields had been inebriated."

Evie slumped back on the chair.

Tom continued, "An empty bottle of brandy was found in Mr. Prentiss' room by the balcony. Mr. Prentiss had purchased it as a gift for one of his clients. The detective thinks May Fields came across it and drank it."

Evie murmured, "I find that hard to believe."

"Why am I not surprised?"

"Well, think about it. It is all very convenient. Not only is she labeled a drunk, she is also a thief. Meanwhile, poor Mr. Prentiss is the victim of theft."

"I take it this makes no difference and you wish to continue your pursuit of justice for May Fields."

Evie lifted her chin. "You're darned right." She surged to her feet and made a beeline for the door. "I think it might be best if you order the whiskey and bring it up to my room. I wouldn't wish to be labeled a drunk."

"Evie."

"I… I am in shock and a good stiff drink will do me a world of good." She left the manager's office and went straight to her room. Once there, she went to stand by the window to gaze out to sea.

"I find this all too convenient," she murmured under her breath.

A short while later, Tom appeared and set a bottle of whiskey down. "Are you still annoyed by the news?"

"Yes, pour me that drink, please."

Tom poured the drink and handed her the glass.

Evie waved the glass under her nose and considered downing the whiskey in one go the way she'd seen her granny do many times. Instead, she took a small sip.

"It doesn't make sense." She shook her head and turned toward the view of the sea. "We know May Fields was a hard worker and never missed a day of work. That makes her as honest as they come. Why would she stoop so low?"

"Perhaps there is something to your theory about a liaison between May and Mr. Prentiss," Tom suggested.

Evie swung toward Tom. "What if someone is trying to cover this up? The manager. The hotel owner. I imagine the manager must have contacted him straightaway. The owner would not have wanted the reputation of his new hotel to be besmirched by a scandal so he contrived a way to blame the maid."

Tom sat down on the edge of a chair. "It's quite feasible."

"Female sensitivities," Evie muttered. "If the Worthing detective had wanted to spare me, he might have taken you aside and told you in private. Instead, the information comes to light now when he knows I have gone ahead and contacted another detective."

"Are you now suggesting the Worthing detective is responsible for some sort of cover-up?"

"I wouldn't put it past him." Evie took an angry sip of her drink.

A knock at the door was followed by Caro's entrance. "Milady. I thought I saw you headed upstairs. Earlier, I thought I saw you going out so Edmonds and

I followed you but then we lost you, so we had afternoon tea."

"Did you find out something, Caro?"

"I did, milady." Caro looked from Evie's glass to Tom's glass.

"Oh, I have just had some unpleasant news." Evie filled her in and watched Caro gasp in surprise.

"No. Drunk?" Caro gave a fierce shake of her head. "That can't be right. The maid I spoke with insists May Fields was a hard worker and extremely efficient. They both worked together. In fact, they cleaned Mr. Prentiss' room together. That's the rule in this hotel. All the maids work in pairs. Anyhow, when they finished, they left together and moved onto the next room. Then, May Fields returned to the room because the other maid said she'd forgotten to change the soap. By then, they'd already finished for the day. May offered to run back and do it herself."

"And it was the other maid who remembered not changing the soap?"

"Yes."

So, May Fields had returned to the room.

"What time would this have been?"

Caro smiled. "I asked her about that. They finished at exactly midday. That's when she told me about being efficient. They have so many rooms to clean, they have to keep to a schedule and it was May's afternoon off and she had plans to go to her favorite tea room. So they made sure to finish on time."

Midday.

Evie remembered they had arrived at the hotel

shortly after midday. She had then come straight to her room and had fallen asleep soon after. Then, Caro had woken her up at about two in the afternoon.

"There's a two-hour gap." Evie explained her theory. "We arrived at the tea room and Mr. Prentiss and his wife were already there, but we don't know when they arrived." Or... When they had left, she thought.

Tom set his glass down. "I saw the Prentiss couple leave the hotel." He brushed a hand across his eyes. "I can't say for sure what time, but I know I'd been sitting in the lobby for a short while. So, it must have been just after midday."

And definitely before she and Tom had left the hotel.

When Evie and Tom had finished their afternoon tea, they had then gone for a walk along the pier and Mr. Prentiss and his wife had still been at the tea room. But they must have left some time after...

"Do you remember anything else about the Prentiss couple?" Evie asked. "Did they come down the stairs or had they already been downstairs, perhaps in the library?"

Tom shook his head. "I only saw them when they stepped out through the front doors."

"We need to return to the tea room and see if anyone can tell us what time Mr. Prentiss and his wife left."

Tom checked his watch.

"Yes. Yes. It's too late today. We'll do it first thing tomorrow..."

CHAPTER 11

"*R*etrace May Fields' steps," Evie murmured under her breath.

"How is your fish?" Tom asked.

Distracted from her thoughts, Evie looked up. "Do you remember telling me about your pacing in the lobby?"

Tom looked down at her dish.

"Oh, the fish is fine. I'm more interested in what you said about finding an article in the newspaper interesting. What was it about?" She vaguely remembered him mentioning a murder case...

"Oh, that..." He dropped his gaze and smiled. "The article wrapped up a story about a murder investigation in London. Detective Inspector O'Neill had been mentioned."

"I wish I'd known. I would have congratulated him and... As I recall, you had made a point of telling me I had become fixated with murder and there you were, reading an article about a murder case to entertain you when nothing else had been able to hold your interest for long."

"Feeling better now?"

Evie gave him a brilliant smile. "Yes, thank you." Could she now use that as a way to justify her continued interest in May Fields' death? News about the maid's state of inebriation had more or less convinced Tom she had fallen to her death. However, Evie couldn't let it go.

He sipped his wine and studied her over the rim of the glass. "You're still obsessing about it."

Evie felt she had good reason to obsess. It took her mind off feeling cross with the police for withholding that vital piece of information. If she had known about May's state of inebriation, she would have asked her friend, Ruth Charles, about it. Evie would bet anything Ruth would have told them May Fields had never touched a drop of alcohol in her life. Yes, there could always be a first time. If that had been May's first time drinking, she had certainly made up for it. Who could imbibe an entire bottle of hard liquor?

Tom laughed. "You're even thinking about it right now."

Evie felt her cheeks growing warm so she didn't see the point in denying it. "Yes, I've been thinking about May Fields. Why did she go into the Prentiss couple's room alone when the hotel imposes a rule against maids going into rooms by themselves?"

"Because she was pressed for time. She wanted to get on with her free half day."

"That's what I don't understand. Why not ask the other maid to change the soap?"

"Because May Fields is hard working and conscientious?"

Evie glanced at her watch and wondered how Caro had fared. While she'd dressed for dinner, she had asked her maid to follow the Prentiss couple and to keep the task to herself. Although, she had given her leave to share it with Edmonds. But she had made a point of excluding Tom from the plans.

She sensed he would disapprove of her continued interest in the odd couple. Now, however, he knew she had not abandoned her suspicions.

Raising his glass to his lips, Tom murmured, "The Addington couple have been shown to a table just to your right. They still look happy. I'm surprised you haven't included them in your suspicions."

"I thought you had decided there was nothing worth pursuing."

"The police seem to know what they are doing."

"And that is good enough for you?" Evie didn't bother hiding her surprise. "I thought you knew better by now."

"Yes, well... You seem to enjoy dabbling, so I thought you might appreciate having the Addington couple pointed out." Tom sighed. "Fine. While the police appear to be content with their findings, I believe you have reason to be suspicious."

"What changed your mind?"

"Nothing in particular. I am merely putting my trust in you. While I think it would be better if you left it alone and tried to enjoy your vacation, I can see you enjoy drawing character portraits."

"Oh, that's an interesting way of referring to what we've been doing." Evie studied the couple in question. "But how could I possibly link them to May's death?" Evie laughed. "While I am prepared to employ my imagination to sketch a theory, I realize there are limits."

"I believe the police could learn a thing or two from you," Tom offered. "As we know, they work with facts, but now I'm thinking it wouldn't hurt to use some creativity."

A waiter cleared their plates and served their desserts.

"My compliments to the chef," Evie offered. "That fish was cooked to perfection." Evie scooped up some ice cream and savored it.

"Mr. Addington is a banker and Mr. Prentiss is a lawyer," Tom said. "How difficult would it be to link them together?"

"Tom, I believe you are teasing me."

Tom finished his wine and set his glass down. "Indulge me for a moment."

"Great. Now you are going to encourage me."

"No, it's now my turn to sketch out a scenario."

"Wouldn't you rather talk about flint mines?" Evie followed his gaze. The Addington couple were holding up champagne glasses. The wife smiled while her husband murmured sweet nothings. "So, what's on your mind?"

Tom leaned forward. "The banker and the lawyer

are not here at the same time by accident. They're in cahoots and... they're here to work out the details. What do lawyers do?" Tom didn't wait for Evie to answer. "They deal with estate business. They look after people's interests. Draw up wills." His eyes brightened. "Both the banker and the lawyer have information about wealthy widows with no one to leave their money to."

Getting into the spirit of the game, Evie suggested, "And they are conspiring to... introduce those wealthy widows to scoundrel gentlemen who will steal all their money?"

"Or the lawyer could be skimming off his clients and the banker could be helping him hide the money."

"In which case, Mr. and Mrs. Prentiss should be in a happy mood, but they're not." Evie swirled her spoon around the ice cream. "I think there must be something more wicked going on. The banker could be blackmailing the lawyer." Evie glanced around the restaurant. "I don't see the Prentiss couple. Have you noticed if both couples have been in the same room at the same time?"

"On the first day, we saw them both at the tea room."

"Oh, yes. I remember now." And she would soon know where Mr. Prentiss and his wife had chosen to spend the evening because she knew she could trust Caro with the task of trailing after them. "I think you might be right. They are working together and Mr. Prentiss is not happy about it."

"Because he's getting the raw end of the deal," Tom

suggested. Brushing his finger over his chin, he added, "This might be stretching and pushing the bounds of possibilities but what if they are both working for the hotel owner?"

"Now, there's an idea." Evie straightened. "The hotel owner takes care of luring wealthy widows to his hotel…" Evie took a deep swallow. "I'm a wealthy widow."

They stared at each other for long seconds without blinking.

"They're in the process of setting me up to extort money from me."

"Blackmail," Tom mused.

Evie could actually see the possibility taking shape in her mind. Her granny's worst nightmare and the reason she had hired Tom…

His eyebrows slammed together. "Here's a connection. Every time we have been together, one or both couples have been present."

Evie scooped up some ice cream only to set her spoon down. "No one could have known we would go to the tea room on the first day." Seeing the couples at the tea room had been nothing but a coincidence. "It couldn't be blackmail. I lead a simple life. I do nothing that could be used against me."

"You travel around with a man who used to be your chauffeur and is now parading around as your friend. Some people might find that suspicious and worth exploiting for their own nefarious purposes."

"Okay, so how does all that tie in with May Fields?" Evie asked.

"We need coffee." Tom looked around and gained the attention of a waiter who promptly delivered some hot coffee. "We have already considered the possibility May Fields overheard something or saw something."

"And they got rid of her?" Evie glanced at the Addington couple. "If they had conspired to kill May, would they be able to enjoy themselves as they have been?"

"If they're cold-blooded enough." Tom nodded. "I don't see why not."

Evie stirred some sugar into her coffee and studied Mr. Hector Addington. "Would you say he has a prominent jaw?"

"It looks regular to me. Dare I ask?"

Evie considered ignoring the prompt. Sighing, she said, "If you must know, before we set off on our trip, I had been reading a book by an Italian criminologist."

"Is that a real word?"

"Yes, he coined it. Anyhow, the author argues that criminals have certain defining physical characteristics."

"A prominent jaw being one of them?"

Evie nodded. "A prominent jaw. Widely separated cheekbones and thick dark hair."

They both turned and looked at Mr. Hector Addington.

"What time did we return to the hotel the day May Fields died?" Evie asked.

"It must have been around five in the afternoon."

Once they had left the tea room, they had lost track of the Addington couple. They could have returned to the hotel, done the deed and then blended in with the crowd or the hotel guests. Evie played around with the idea and realized there was a huge gap in time between the moment May Fields went into the Prentiss hotel room and the moment she jumped to her death from the same room.

Also, how did Mr. Addington gain access to Mr. Prentiss' room? Evie shook her head and reminded herself they had decided the two men had banded together.

Yes, but…

Had May Fields spent the entire afternoon drinking herself into a stupor?

She stared at her coffee and pictured May Fields wallowing in self-pity because she had been duped by Mr. Prentiss to believe he would leave his wife for her. Seeing the couple returning to the hotel together, she finally understood there would not be a happy-ever-after ending for her, so she decided to end it all…

That was one theory. Evie switched her thoughts to their other theory. May Fields had overheard something…

But why would she steal the brandy and stay in Mr. Prentiss' room to drink it?

"Motive," Tom said.

Abandoning her theory about the brokenhearted May Fields, she focused on their previous theory. "May saw or overheard something that implicated the Addington couple and the Prentiss couple in some sort of conspiracy. They might have been planning to trap a wealthy widow or, as you suggested, they might be stealing money from clients." Evie's lip kicked up. "Caro said the maid told her she and May Fields finished cleaning the Prentiss room and then they moved onto another room. Then, May had to go back to the Prentiss room. Now, picture this... The Prentiss couple returned. They found May in the room and Mr. Prentiss decided to use the opportunity to get rid of her..." Evie pushed out a breath. "No. The timing is still not right. May went into the room at midday and she died close to five in the afternoon." Evie shook her head. "I've considered this possibility before and reached the same conclusion." So, why had she revisited the idea?

"Cognac?" Tom asked.

"Yes, I think I need to dull my senses otherwise I will spend the night tossing and turning." Evie drummed her fingers on the table. "And during my tossing and turning, I will most likely come up with something along the lines of Mr. Prentiss or Mr. Addington killed May at midday, went out to make sure they were seen in public, then they returned to the hotel and threw her body over the balcony at five in the afternoon."

"I think Phillipa would love your theory," Tom said. "You must share it with her."

Smiling, Evie thought of her Australian friend. She had traveled to London to work on a play with a group of scriptwriters who had recently stayed at Halton House. Yes, she would definitely enjoy the tale.

Looking up, she saw Caro hovering by the dining room entrance. Evie signaled for her to join them.

Caro looked around and then made a beeline for their table.

Tom surged to his feet and drew a chair out for Caro.

"Edmonds and I have only just returned from our dinner." Caro winked at Evie.

"Should I leave you two alone?" Tom asked.

"Oh, he might as well know." Evie's eyes danced around Tom's face. "I asked Caro to follow the Prentiss couple."

"To what end?"

Evie shrugged. "Curiosity. They don't appear to be here to have fun so there must be another reason for their trip to Worthing."

"I'm sorry to say I didn't see them doing anything suspicious," Caro said. "They barely spoke during their meal. Half the time I'm sure they were not even looking at each other. I don't think they're happy."

hen Caro entered Evie's room the next morning, she found Evie having breakfast in bed.

Seeing Caro's surprised expression, Evie said, "I feel I should apologize. While I am not known for lounging around in bed in the morning having breakfast, I am on vacation." And feeling reluctant to face another day of unanswered questions, Evie thought. Taking a sip of her tea, she murmured, "If you must know, I am lacking motivation and direction."

"You need to come up with a solid lead, milady. I am on your side and wholeheartedly agree with you. May Fields did not kill herself."

"What makes you so certain?" Evie asked.

"I'm not sure I can put it into words... but I'll try. When you go into service, you don't question it. You simply accept your lot in life. You say to yourself, this is what I can do, so I will do it and count my blessings."

"But not everyone who goes into services stays there,"

Evie said. In recent times, many people working in service had moved on to take other positions working as sales people and in factories because the conditions were either better, with less working hours, or they paid better.

Caro paced around the room and stopped. "We are practical. That's what I am trying to say. Even if May Fields entertained fanciful ideas about having afternoon tea and pretending to be a grand lady, she would have seen that as a temporary escape and then returned to her life feeling satisfied."

"So, in your opinion, she would not have gone overboard with her aspirations." And she would not have allowed herself to be duped by a married man, Evie thought.

"That's right. I think she would have remained well grounded. Even if something had happened with Mr. Prentiss, she would have found a way to move past it."

Were people in service really a breed unto themselves, made of sterner stuff?

"Caro, do you think there are exceptions?"

Caro turned and looked out of the window. "Yes, I suppose there are… Well, so much for trying to give you a better understanding of my world."

"Oh, but you did."

Caro continued, "As much as I would like to think she didn't allow her flights of fancy to become her own undoing, it would be silly to ignore the alternative. So, we must be practical and also consider the possibility May Fields was the exception and she meant to do something about changing her life." Caro gave a firm nod. "But then something happened. Maybe she fell in with the wrong people."

"It's interesting that you should say that. Last night, Tom and I came up with some new ideas. The wildest of which sees the maid being killed at midday and then being thrown over the balcony in the afternoon." She watched Caro's reaction to the news.

"That sounds like a lot of hard work," Caro said. "Why would a murderer go to all that trouble?"

"To throw the police off their trail. They would have made sure they were seen in public, thereby providing themselves with a solid alibi."

"But they would have needed to return to the hotel to throw the body over the balcony."

Evie set her breakfast tray aside and slumped back against her pillow to think. A moment later, she flung the bedcovers off. "That is our task for the day. We must ask simply everyone for help in placing Mr. Prentiss and his wife. In fact, I'd already mentioned this to Tom." She tapped her chin in thought. "Yes, I said we needed to return to the tea room and ask if anyone had noticed when the Prentiss couple had left. We will map out their progress throughout the day. I specifically want to know when they returned to the hotel. Someone must have seen them. That way, I'm sure we will find a gap, meaning a moment of opportunity, and I am willing to bet that gap will be around the time May Fields fell to her death."

"But why? I mean... Why would Mr. Prentiss kill the maid?"

Evie told her about the new theories she and Tom had come up with the previous evening.

"Oh, I like this new theory. Mr. Prentiss is running some sort of scam with Mr. Addington and the maid witnessed or heard something she should not have."

"Precisely."

"Do you think that's why Mr. Prentiss looks so morose?"

A knock at the door had Caro rushing to answer it. A bellboy handed her a piece of paper. Closing the door, Caro approached the bed and handed Evie the note.

"Oh, my man of business telephoned and wants me to return the call. Fabulous. I hope he has some good news. Is Tom up and about?"

"He had breakfast in the dining room with Edmonds and then he went to the library to read the newspapers. He said he'll wait for you there."

Caro held up a dress for her inspection, making Evie wonder what one should wear when trying to flush out a murderer.

After making use of the manager's office to contact her man of business, Evie went in search of Tom. She walked with purpose and, most likely, looked like a woman on a mission. The brim of her blue and white boat hat sat a fraction above her eyes so she had to tip her head back slightly to see where she was going.

When she didn't find Tom in the lobby, she remembered Caro mentioning he had settled down in the library. Stopping a bellboy, she asked for directions. Evie followed his instructions and headed toward the back of the building where a spacious room had been set up as the library. She found Tom sitting on a leather winged armchair.

The library had a row of windows facing a small garden on a terrace to the side of the building and provided ample natural light. However, there were also several table lamps scattered around. In Evie's opinion, the dark wood paneling made it the perfect retreat for gentlemen. When she caught a whiff of cigar smoke, she decided some of the gentlemen had taken it upon themselves to claim the room as their own.

Seeing her, Tom set his newspaper aside and made a point of looking at his watch.

"My apologies. To be clear, it did not take me this long to dress." Evie sat down on a chair next to him. Looking around, she noticed another gentleman sitting in a corner. He appeared to be immersed in a book but she didn't want anyone overhearing their conversation.

"Let's take a walk... to the pier."

"This must be serious and you must be desperate." Tom's eyebrows lifted. "Also, I see you are playing it safe with your hat today."

"Yes, I decided to avoid wearing anything that might prove too tempting for the seagulls. It's a boat hat. Do you like it?"

He tapped his fedora hat against his hand and then settled it on his head. "I'm glad I don't have that many choices at my disposal. If I did, it would take me as long as… Never mind. Yes, I do like it." He lowered his head, "But I can barely see your eyes."

"I know. It adds an air of mystery." Stepping out of the library, she whispered, "Say something amusing." Before he could speak, she tipped her head back and laughed.

When they exited the hotel, Tom said, "You're about to enlighten me and share the joke."

"Oh, I was pretending to be like everyone else. You know, faking my *joie de vivre*."

"Faking. Why?"

"So no one could see I'm actually up to something."

"And… Are you up to something?"

Evie made him wait until they reached the end of the pier.

Tom leaned against the railing and looked out to sea. "Since we appear to be trying to avoid detection, I'm pretending to be admiring the sea and trying to avoid thinking about your state of mind."

Evie looked around to make sure there was no one standing close enough to overhear their conversation. "You're not going to like this."

"You have my attention."

"Well, yesterday I kept thinking about the detective's advice to retrace May Fields' day." But then Tom had distracted her, Evie thought.

"And?"

"No one saw her in the afternoon. In fact, the moment she went into the Prentiss room, she might as well have disappeared in a puff of smoke."

Tom turned around and crossed his arms. "Isn't that

where we left off? No one saw her because she stayed in that room to drink the contents of a bottle of… what was it? Brandy?"

"We can use that information to our advantage. Since we have been led to believe May Fields spend the afternoon in Mr. Prentiss' hotel room getting drunk, we know Mr. Prentiss was not in the hotel. At least, not until five in the afternoon. Today, we are going to find out where he and his wife were. Even if we have to approach them and get the information from them ourselves."

"But we already know they were in the tea room."

"Aha! But only until we left."

Tom tipped his hat back. "You sound determined."

"That's because I am." Lowering her voice, she said, "I have saved the best information until last. Earlier, I spoke with my man of business. Mr. Matthew Keys has more than earned his keep. He has traced Mr. Prentiss' steps and you will never guess which village he visited earlier in the year."

"Findon."

"Oh, you guessed."

"What took him there?"

"He had a legitimate reason. He went there alone to settle an estate matter." Evie waited for the information to sink in.

"And?"

"Brace yourself."

Tom leaned back against the railing. "I'm as ready as I will ever be."

Evie counted to three. "Earlier in the year, May Fields was still working and living in Findon."

"Are you sure?"

"Well... No. But I have charged Caro with the task of finding out when May came to work at the hotel and I know the information she will provide will match my suspicions. May Fields met Mr. Prentiss in Findon earlier in the year."

"I see. You have made a link without verifying your information."

"That's only a minor detail soon to be rectified."

"At the risk of repeating myself... And?"

"Don't you see? It's our first solid link. My man of business is continuing his investigation. I asked him to focus on finding a connection between Mr. Prentiss and Mr. Addington. There's bound to be one."

"Even though we haven't seen them together? You would think if they knew each other, they'd spend time together."

Evie gave a firm nod. "Unless they didn't want anyone to know they are acquainted." Evie folded her arms and tapped her foot. "I think this is the sort of information we should share with the police but I fear they will not be interested. Certainly not until we can provide solid proof of wrongdoing."

"So, how do you wish to proceed? I take it you have already made plans for us today."

"We need to visit the tea room."

They made their way there. Despite their eagerness to learn more, they took their time to appreciate the day. Out of curiosity, Evie searched for straw hats with fruit on them while Tom whistled a soft tune.

Halfway there, he asked, "What makes you think anyone will remember Mr. and Mrs. Prentiss? If we hadn't recognized them from the hotel, I doubt we would have noticed them at all."

Evie didn't want to admit it, but Tom had made a good point. She would not have noticed them. "How would you have described them if we'd seen them anywhere else, under different circumstances?"

"Nondescript. Apart from the fact they both look lifeless, they have no features that stand out."

"And yet, the first time I saw him in the hotel lobby, when he sat by himself, I recall thinking he looked like a *bon vivant*. Perhaps he looks better when he is alone," Evie said. "What if his appearance looked different because he hadn't yet killed the maid?"

"Maybe he'd been happy about something else. We haven't been able to find out if the woman with him is his wife. I've asked the concierge but he couldn't confirm it. Remember, there is some doubt about their status, which would explain something."

"Would it?" Evie gave him a brisk smile. "Let me guess. He is now unhappy with his paramour. If he is having some sort of affair, you'd think he would be with someone he wanted to be with. Unless, the initial attraction has now faded and he has come to realize he has made a mistake but he is stuck with her."

"Oh, yes." Tom laughed under his breath. "Now that almost explains their obvious unhappiness."

"Only if they are not involved in some sort of evil deed."

Tom agreed with a pensive nod. "Let's hope someone at the tea room noticed them." Cupping Evie's elbow, he guided them across the street. "What do you have planned for the rest of the day?"

"You'll be pleased to hear I wish to drive back to Findon. The way you are bound to drive, we should arrive there well before lunch. After the tea room, we'll return to the hotel where I will contact my man of business for an update and then we shall set off. Is that agreeable with you?" Seeing Tom's surprise, Evie laughed. "You didn't expect me to ask. Anyone would think I pull the strings."

"You sort of do."

As they came up to the tea room, they scanned the street.

"I don't see them leaving or heading toward the tea room," Tom said. "Now to see if they are inside."

"And if they are, we have simply come for some refreshments and we will have to employ our outmost discretion when making inquiries about them," Evie said.

A swift glance inside the tea room was enough to determine the couple were not there.

"Do you recognize any of the waiters?" Tom asked.

"Not even if my life depended on it. What does that say about me? I'm not the type of person to look down my nose at people in service. Considering how much effort I have been putting into noticing people, you would think I'd remember a face."

"If it makes you feel any better, Countess, I don't remember any of the waiters either. I think we will have to be creative." He gestured toward a table. "At least we get to sit down for a cup of coffee."

A waiter approached them, settled them down at their table and took their order.

As they placed their order, Evie made a point of making eye contact with him and smiling.

Tom laughed under his breath. "You're overcompensating."

"I am not. I'm merely being my usual, polite self. Fine, yes... I'm trying to make up for any past omissions. Although, I'm sure I'm always polite. Just not observant enough to remember a waiter's face."

"Here he comes," Tom whispered.

"You'd think we're trying to extricate a state secret." Evie sat back and let Tom do the talking. Despite his precise description of Mr. and Mrs. Prentiss, he failed to trigger the waiter's memory.

"Are waiters assigned to specific tables?" When the waiter nodded, Evie added, "Recently, Mr. and Mrs. Prentiss sat at the next table..."

"Oh, Yes. Mr. Prentiss."

Evie and Tom exchanged a look of surprise.

"You have heard of him."

"Certainly, but only because he left his business card."

"When did this happen?" Evie asked.

The waiter looked up for a moment. "Oh, the day of the accident at a nearby hotel. That would be two days ago."

"And do you remember what time they left?"

Unfortunately, the waiter couldn't say for sure but he offered to ask around.

"Can you believe he left his business card? The man is on vacation and still thinking about work." Or, she thought, he might have been trying to establish his whereabouts at a specific time. She didn't get a chance to share her suspicion with Tom because he beat her to it.

"If he handed the card to someone close to five in the afternoon, he would have given himself a solid alibi."

The waiter returned and said, "Four forty-five. The waiter who served them remembered the time because Mr. Prentiss actually asked him. Apparently, his watch was running slow."

Evie thanked him. She poured the tea and took her time sipping it.

"Well," Tom said.

"Yes. Well…"

"Are we both astonished?" Tom asked.

"We must be."

"And yet, it is exactly the sort of information you wanted to hear."

Evie set her teacup down. "If we ask around the nearby businesses, I am willing to bet Mr. Prentiss did not distribute his cards around."

"I agree. Mr. Prentiss only wanted his precise whereabouts known on that day at that time. But I suppose we should be thorough and ask around.

Remember, if you wish to approach the police, you will need to provide evidence of your suspicions."

"It will take too long," Evie mused. "We need to drive to Findon. I suggest waiting until we return or if we find Caro and Edmonds at the hotel we can ask them to look into it."

Tom dug inside his coat and drew out a small pocket book.

She watched him write down a couple of names. "Are you taking notes?"

Tom nodded. "I think we should try to find out what time the Prentiss couple left the hotel. I only know it was after midday."

It took a moment for the information to sink in. If Mr. Prentiss had a solid alibi, they were without a suspect. Which meant they had to look elsewhere...

CHAPTER 13

"Country clubs," Evie mused as they made their way to Findon.

"Pardon? I missed that."

"I'm not surprised. Your attention is on the road, as it should be." Leaning in, Evie said, "There are no country clubs here. At least, none that I can think of. Back home, they seem to be everywhere. And, now that I think about it, I have already discussed this. So much for trying to keep myself entertained while the scenery whizzes by me."

"I believe you had actually talked about resort towns."

"Oh, yes. You're right."

"Do you want a country club?"

"No. I only noticed the absence of them."

"Instead of country clubs, you have other people's private estates to visit."

Evie laughed. "Are you mocking our way of life?"

"I wouldn't dream of it and I don't really have a reason to. If I wanted to mock you, I would comment on the amount of luggage you insist on taking with you, but I've only ever seen you traveling light."

"That's because we haven't been up north yet. I should plan a trip for the shooting season."

"What should I look forward to seeing?"

"An entourage." Evie laughed. "But nothing compared to what we would do back home. Caro would be mortified... Well, surprised, by the extravagance of what we refer to as a camping trip. When the J.P. Morgans of the world go camping, they take their entire household to the wilderness. I heard say a real estate millionaire from Brooklyn fenced off 8,600 acres and built a château and called it his camping ground. Granny told me in her last missive, Marjorie Meriweather Post set up the ultimate camping ground, with sixty-eight buildings and a staff of eighty plus. She had her guests ferried in by yachts and her own train."

Tom changed gears and slowed down.

During most of the drive to Findon, they had both been silent. Evie assumed Tom had been mulling over what they had learned.

Earlier, when they had returned to the hotel, Evie had rushed upstairs to change clothes, leaving Tom to talk with the concierge.

What he had discovered had left them both speechless.

On the day May Fields had died, Mr. Prentiss had talked with the concierge before leaving for lunch. He had specifically asked the time because, according to him, his watch had been running slow.

Either the man was fixated with time or he had made a deliberate effort to place himself in a specific place at a specific time. Not once, but twice.

Evie straightened her hat and said, "Since you're not going to say it, I will. Mr. Prentiss is guilty of something. I'm just not sure what he might have done."

"Killed the maid, of course." Tom brought the roadster to a stop just outside the village.

"If he killed the maid, he must be confident no one will find out. Otherwise, he would have made his getaway. Heavens, he has even remained in the same room. In his place, I would have either returned home or requested another room."

Tom gave her his hand and she stepped out of the roadster.

"If we are to uncover anything worthwhile, we will have to keep a closer eye on him."

"Isn't Caro following him around?"

"Yes. She says she is enjoying herself, but I can't help thinking she would much rather be doing something else. She will also ask around and see if Mr. Prentiss left his business card anywhere else."

When they reached the tea room, Evie pointed at the sign. "It's also a guest house. I hadn't noticed that before."

"How did your man of business unearth the information about Mr. Prentiss visiting Findon?"

"He actually thought it would take longer but he is

well connected. Also, he appears to know how to use his resources. First, he located the office Mr. Prentiss works at. Then, he sent his assistant to make an appointment to see Mr. Prentiss. In the process, he befriended Mr. Prentiss' secretary. From what I understand, he is young and rather handsome. I told my man of business I wanted to find a link between Mr. Prentiss and May Fields who had once lived in Findon. His assistant used that to fish around for some relevant information."

"In other words, you pointed him in the right direction."

Evie shrugged. "I must have experienced a moment of clarity. If we're to connect Mr. Prentiss to May Fields, I really don't see the harm in creating the connection first."

Tom tilted his head and studied her. "That is actually a practical way of approaching it. I cannot wait to hear you provide this information to the police."

"Oh, do you really think we'll have the opportunity?"

"If I didn't believe it before, I certainly do so now. Shall we go in?"

The tea room appeared to be hosting a meeting of sorts. Several tables had been joined to form a larger area for nearly a dozen women.

The waitress approached them with a ready smile.

"I hope we are not intruding," Evie said.

"Not at all. The local ladies are hosting their monthly committee meeting."

Evie almost wished they could forgo the need to sit and order something and cut straight to the chase, but if they didn't take the opportunity to eat something now they would miss out on lunch because they wouldn't return to Worthing in time for lunch.

Evie had a brief glance at the menu and set it down. "I'll have whatever you are having."

Turning slightly, Evie studied the group of women. Assuming they had met to discuss some sort of serious matter, it appeared their lunch had taken precedence over it. Perhaps that had been the purpose of their meeting. Evie had attended far too many of them to know they were only ever about serious business but occasionally, the ladies liked to celebrate their achievements.

Hearing one of the ladies calling the waitress by her name, Evie used the information to her advantage. When the waitress brought their meal, Evie smiled. "Abigail. What a lovely name."

"Thank you, milady."

"Abigail, do you remember us from our last visit?" Evie asked.

"Yes, of course, milady."

"You were extremely helpful."

"I'm glad to hear that, milady."

"I wonder if you might be able to help us again."

The waitress nodded.

"You said May Fields had worked here. Was that before you took up your position here?"

Abigail smiled. "She worked through her notice and

then she left, but she stayed around until I could find my way properly."

"So, when did you start your employment here?"

"Six months ago, milady."

"My traveling companion and I only now realized this establishment also serves as a guest house. Do you get many visitors to the area?"

Abigail nodded. "We have regular guests."

Evie wondered if the young girl would be able to identify Mr. Prentiss but she couldn't think how she would describe him. Her initial perception of him differed greatly to how she saw him now. She did, however, have the advantage of knowing when Mr. Prentiss had stayed here. Her man of business had been quite thorough. Or, rather, his assistant had been extremely resourceful and successful in retrieving the information from Mr. Prentiss' secretary.

"Do you remember a Mr. Prentiss staying here?" Evie asked.

Abigail gave it some thought. "The name rings a bell. Mrs. Johnstone would be able to tell you. She's the proprietress."

"Oh, do you think we might be able to speak with her?"

"I'll see if she is available."

Tom nudged her. "This might be a good time to consider adopting an alter ego."

"Pardon?"

"You can't introduce yourself as… yourself. Do you want word to spread about the Countess of Woodridge? What if it gets back to Mr. Prentiss?"

"Oh, I hadn't thought of that. You're suggesting I go incognito."

"Yes."

Evie tried to think of a name and drew a blank. "Heavens. Who could I be?"

"She's coming."

A woman emerged from a back room, her cheeks rosy, her eyes bright. Looking around the tea room, her gaze settled on Tom and Evie and she headed toward them.

"Quick. Quick. What do I call myself?"

"Ms. Crystal Aston," Tom suggested.

Mrs. Johnstone smiled at them and introduced herself.

"How very kind of you to make time for us. This is Mr. W-Winthrop and I am Crystal Astor."

"You're American."

"Why, yes... We are."

"Any relation to the American Astors?"

Tom's foot found Evie's under the table.

Mrs. Johnstone seemed to be impressed at the prospect of hosting a member of the Astor family, so Evie decided to go with it... "Oh... Yes. I'm a distant relative."

Giving Evie a bright smile, Mrs. Johnstone said, "Abigail tells me you were asking about someone."

"A Mr. Prentiss."

Mrs. Johnstone's mouth firmed. "He stayed with us for a short time." Her eyebrow lifted slightly when she said, "I believe he came here for business."

It seemed Mrs. Johnstone believed there had been another purpose to his trip.

Evie lowered her voice, "Was he a disagreeable character?"

Mrs. Johnstone looked over her shoulder before saying, "He tried to chat up one of my waitresses and then he followed her home. I saw him with my own eyes."

"And what did you do?"

Mrs. Johnstone straightened and lifted her chin. "I gave him a piece of my mind and then I asked him to leave."

"And did he?" Evie could not have sounded more intrigued.

Giving a firm nod, Mrs. Johnstone said, "The next day."

"What happened to the waitress?"

Mrs. Johnstone sighed. "She found a new position in Worthing. To this day, I believe Mr. Prentiss had something to do with her leaving. She was my best worker."

"She sounds lovely."

"And she was. I was heartbroken when I heard what happened to her." Mrs. Johnstone excused herself for a moment. When she returned, she held a photograph. "This was taken on her last day here. We threw a little party and posed for a photograph."

Tom and Evie leaned in to study the image, both remarking on her prettiness.

"I look after my girls and I can't help feeling if she had stayed here, she would still be alive today." Mrs.

Johnstone drew out a handkerchief and wiped her nose. "But then, that is life."

Evie thanked the proprietress for her time. Settling back to enjoy her tea she tried to come up with a story for Mr. Prentiss' interest in May Fields other than the obvious one.

"Astor?" Tom murmured.

"Isn't that what you said?"

"No, I said Aston. Like the motor car."

Evie waved her hand in dismissal. "I'm sure there are plenty of Astors around."

"Yes, but you claimed to be a distant relative."

"You worry too much, Mr. Winchester."

"A moment ago, it was Winthrop. Do I look like a Winthrop to you?"

"What's wrong with the name?"

"It sounds stuffy and, considering the shenanigans we have been getting up to lately, I am anything but stuffy. I hope none of this ever gets back to your grandmother. I am supposed to be keeping you out of this type of trouble."

"Never mind all that. What do you suppose Mr. Prentiss wanted with May Fields? Apart from the obvious?"

Tom cupped his chin in his hand. "I honestly couldn't say. He approached her here and then he met her in Worthing. How do you think that encounter went?"

"Are you suggesting we should think of the obvious reason?" Evie gaped. "Wait a minute. He came to Findon alone. What if he did accost her? Several months later, he finds himself in Worthing with his wife and, to his surprise, the maid cleaning his room is the young woman he tried to chat up here."

"She might have tried to confront him about it or, he might have been foolish enough to try again," Tom suggested.

"Let me think. May Fields sees him in the hotel, then she realizes he is staying in the room she has to clean. There is no getting out of it without making a fuss, so she keeps quiet about it. However, at some point, she can no longer bear the idea of this horrible man living the high life and getting away with approaching unmarried women and seducing them. She finds herself in his room. She sees the bottle of brandy…" Evie's shoulders slumped. "If I continue with the story, I'm afraid I will have to say May Fields suffered a bout of self-pity, caved in to temptation or maybe anger. Yes, anger. She snatches the bottle and considers tipping the contents out. Instead, she breaks down and takes a swig of the drink." Evie drummed her fingers on the table. "Help me out."

"There's only one ending to your story. She had one too many sips of the brandy and became quite inebriated. She might have gone out onto the balcony to sober up and that's when she fell."

"Face down. Onto the pavement…" Evie surged to her feet. "We need to return to Worthing."

Tom took care of paying for their drinks and they exited the tea room.

"You are suddenly in a hurry to return," Tom said. "Is there a particular reason?"

"Yes, I'm eager to speak with Edmonds. I remember Caro saying he saw May Fields fall to her death."

"And?"

"I didn't ask at the time. Now, I'm hoping he is over the shock. According to Caro, Edmonds didn't take it well. Anyhow, as morbid as it might sound, I would like to ask him for details."

CHAPTER 14

*B*efore they reached the roadster, Evie changed her mind. "While we're here, I think we should try to speak with May's friend."

"What do you want to ask her?"

"I'm not sure yet."

They doubled back, along the way admiring the pretty cottages lined along the street.

"Have you given any thought to how you will spend the rest of the summer?" Tom asked.

"I don't have to. Everything is organized. I'm hosting a house party and, this time, it will coincide with Toodles' visit. Granny should enjoy the company. There'll be a few actresses taking a break from their performance in London. Phillipa is going to try to attend, but she's not sure she'll be able to get away. Her play is taking precedence and she'll still be in full rehearsal mode. In any case, we'll see her when we go to town for her opening night."

Tom hummed under his breath.

"Tom, if you have something to say, then I suggest you verbalize it."

"Actors? You only recently hosted a group of writers. Are you in the process of setting up an artistic salon?"

The fact he knew about salons surprised Evie.

"There'll be other people as well. In fact, you'll be pleased to know there will be several gentlemen present."

Tom grinned. "How gentle will they be?"

"You mean, how snooty? One of them is a newspaper owner. A self-made man."

"Will I be expected to dust off my alter ego?"

"The American millionaire who struck it lucky in the Oklahoma oil fields? Sure, that will be fun. What do you think Toodles will make of him... or, rather, you."

"Toodles is used to my alter ego."

Because... Evie wanted to ask, but where Tom Winchester was concerned, she felt the less she knew, the better. Evie had no idea why she felt that way. If she had to provide a reason, she would probably say there had been enough changes in her life and she needed to enjoy something that felt constant. Tom Winchester provided that, in a strange sort of way.

"Will you be taking your butler to London?"

"Of course. I would never dream of depriving Edgar."

"And you're not afraid he'll want to stay on in London?"

Evie sighed. Edgar had originally been her London butler, but since her country house butler had retired, she had done everything in her power to convince Edgar to stay on in the country. "He's quite content at Halton House." More so now that he and Millicent had formed a strong attachment. Her other maid had been only too happy to leave the town house and settle in the country because, in her opinion, she'd been missing out on all the excitement. "Edgar would never dream of disrupting our happy household."

Evie picked up her pace. "I think that's Ruth Charles. She just came out of the house with the yellow roses." The young woman's reaction didn't differ from the first time they had met her. Evie knew the precise moment when Ruth Charles saw them. Her step faltered. She looked over her shoulder and then, she appeared to push out a breath of resignation.

"Have you thought about what you will ask her?"

"I am hoping May Fields confided in her." She must have, Evie thought and waved. "Hello. We meet again."

They were only a few steps away, close enough to see Ruth Charles bite the edge of her lip.

Evie imagined her wondering what the strange woman could possibly want from her now.

"This is going to sound rather odd," Evie said.

Ruth Charles hugged her basket against her and nodded.

"We heard a rumor about a certain Mr. Prentiss showing an interest in May Fields." Evie watched for her reaction. She thought she saw a slight tinge rise up in her cheeks. "Mrs. Johnstone from the tea room said she saw Mr. Prentiss following May home. Did she tell you about it?"

"She mentioned something. May thought he was trying to get fresh with her so she gave him his marching orders, saying she wasn't that type of girl."

Lowering her voice, Evie asked, "Did she tell you what he wanted from her?"

"He promised her a job."

Evie wanted to clap her hands with joy. They'd found their connection. Mr. Prentiss had known May Fields.

"Did he say what type of job he had in mind?"

"No, but he promised it would be worth her while." Ruth took a step back. "I'm sorry. I really must be going. I'm supposed to be running an errand."

Evie drew out a card and wrote down her man of business' contact number. "If you remember anything, could you please call this number?"

Ruth Charles looked perplexed. "What more do you want to know?"

"You might remember something else that slipped your mind now. For instance, he might have tried to contact her again or he might have sent her a letter."

Ruth Charles gave a stiff nod and walked away.

"I don't think she cared for your line of questioning," Tom said.

Evie's eyebrows drew down. "Did I come on too strong?"

"Well, you sort of left out all the pleasantries and cut straight to the chase."

"You think I should have sweet-talked her? But that would be dishonest."

"And yet, I'm sure Detective Inspector O'Neill excels at sweet-talking confessions out of criminals."

"I'm sure you're teasing me." She took hold of his arm and tugged him along. "Come on. If you drive fast enough, we'll make it back to Worthing in time for a late luncheon."

"In other words, giddy-up." Tom laughed.

"I'm sorry. Should I have sweet-talked you into driving fast?" She settled into the passenger seat and focused on what they had learned.

However, the drive back to Worthing took less time than expected. Certainly not enough for Evie to come up with a foolproof plan for extricating information from Mr. Prentiss.

When Tom slowed down, Evie realized she'd had her eyes closed. Straightening, she said, "What? What's wrong? Why are you slowing down?"

"There's a motor car approaching."

Adjusting her hat, Evie focused on the vehicle. "Is there a protocol? Do we wave?"

"Why would you care?"

Shrugging, Evie said, "It might be someone who recognizes me and if I don't acknowledge them, it might get back to Henrietta and she'll want to know why I've snubbed them. News about it will spread and before you know it, I'll be the talk of the town and be labeled the snobbish Countess."

"Then you should play it safe and issue a cheery wave."

As the other motor car drove by, Evie gasped. "Oh, I

recognize him. It's Mr. Addington. I wonder where he's going? I didn't see Mrs. Addington."

"The plot thickens," Tom teased.

A moment later, Tom slowed down again.

"Another motor car?"

"Yes, and one I recognize. It's Edmonds in your *Duesenberg*."

"What could he be doing out here? Heavens, you don't suppose something has happened to Caro and he's come out searching for us."

Tom brought the roadster to a stop and Evie could see Edmonds slowing down too.

When he reached them, he greeted them with a worried look. "Milady."

"Edmonds, where is Caro?"

Edmonds raked his fingers through his hair. "She's keeping tabs on Mr. Prentiss. When we saw Mr. Addington drive off by himself, she suggested I follow him."

Evie smiled with relief. "Excellent idea." Evie urged him on with a wave.

Tom shifted gears and got them back on the road again. "Now your chauffeur has joined the game too."

"Yes, and I'll have to wait to question him about what he saw when the maid fell. That should give me a chance to sort out the information we have."

Tom changed gears again and the roadster picked up speed.

Evie yelped. "I guess I better hold onto to my hat lest all my thoughts fly away with it."

CHAPTER 15

"*I* must say, Caro has embraced the spirit of our investigation. It would never have occurred to me to send Edmonds chasing after Mr. Addington," Evie remarked when they reached Worthing.

Grinning, Tom said, "You've become contagious."

In a good way, she hoped. "I've been thinking…"

Tom steered Evie away from the path of a couple determined to claim the sidewalk as their own.

"I need to start thinking like a killer."

Tom cleared his throat. "In case you are wondering, I lock my door every night."

"As do I, of course. Just because I feel I need to start thinking like a killer doesn't imply I will begin to act like one."

Keeping his tone light, Tom said, "I'm sure there is a very fine line. How will you keep yourself from crossing it?"

"You jest."

"Do you blame me? I feel you are about to trek down a rabbit hole and drag us all along with you."

Evie's eyes widened with surprise. "You have read *Lewis Caroll?*"

"With the exception of a few intrusive moments of excitement, I have been leading a sedentary lifestyle in the country. There is nothing but time and I choose to spend it wisely."

"I'm glad to hear that. Anyhow, as I was saying, we need to start thinking like killers."

"Oh, I've been roped in to play a role."

"Why did Mr. Prentiss kill May Fields?"

Tom's eyebrow hitched up. "Are you, by any chance, adopting the guilty until proven innocent tactic?"

"Yes, I think it will prove tremendously useful, making us focus on motives and opportunities and whatnot."

"Whatnot? That sounds dangerous."

Evie elbowed him in the ribs. "Please try to take this seriously. Oh, there's Caro."

"Where?"

"Sitting by the window. She must have Mr. Prentiss in her sights."

They stepped inside the hotel, crossed the lobby and headed toward a sitting area. A waiter was just serving Caro some tea. Seeing them, Caro spoke briskly.

"I just asked for another pot of tea, milady," Caro said.

"Oh, I feel rather dusty from our drive, but I suppose there's no harm in sitting here for a cup of tea." Evie settled down opposite Caro and leaned forward to whisper, "Where is Mr. Prentiss?"

"At the opposite end, milady. He has his back to us. He's been sitting there, drinking coffee and reading the newspaper for the better part of the morning. This is my second pot of tea and I'm almost afraid to get up but get up I must. Excuse me for a moment."

Tom removed his hat and sat down beside Evie. "I've said it before, I will say it again. You have missed your calling."

"Nonsense."

"You're too quick to dismiss your abilities. You have taken a passing concern and followed it through until you discovered something that might lead to the reopening of a case... which was never actually a case to begin with. I look forward to the moment you present your information to the local detective."

"Why do I get the feeling you are amusing yourself at my expense? Go ahead and laugh."

"I wouldn't dare because I know you will have the last laugh. I prefer to be in your corner. Thank you."

Evie took a leisurely sip of her tea. "I'm entertaining a stray thought, which is somewhat related to your comment about me missing my calling. Perhaps I have found an engaging occupation. Just because I am an heiress and a Countess doesn't mean I couldn't take an interest. Others before me have chosen to do more with their time even if they didn't need to. I'm thinking of a prominent New York family, the Van Rensselaers. One of the daughters became a nurse and later on took the veil as a Sister of Charity."

Tom's cup rattled on its saucer. "Are you inclined to follow her footsteps?"

"I don't believe I am as such. My point is, she didn't need to do anything other than enjoy a life of leisure. Her family is incredibly wealthy. Instead, she chose to take an interest." Evie leaned forward and patted his hand. "You look stricken. I'll try to lighten the mood. Did you know the author of *Moby-Dick*, Herman Melville, was related to the Van Rensselaers? In fact, he mentions them in the first chapter of his book. Oh, now that I think of it, Edith Wharton is also related to them. While I haven't yet read her latest novel, *The Age of Innocence*, I've heard say she based the fictional Van der Luydens family on the real Van Rensselaers." Evie looked up and laughed.

"Yes?"

"Oh, I'm just thinking of Henrietta. You know how she dreads calling my granny by her nickname of Toodles. I wonder what she would make of Edith Wharton being known as Pussy Jones to her family?"

Caro returned and noted, "I seem to have missed something."

"Oh, we were merely filling in the time," Evie said. "Now, before I forget, we encountered Edmonds on the road. He appeared to be..." Evie clicked her fingers, "what's the word I'm looking for? Trailing?"

Tom suggested, "Tailing."

"Yes, tailing Mr. Addington."

Caro grinned and said in a hushed tone, "Yes, I decided he looked suspicious."

"What prompted you?"

"He walked past Mr. Prentiss and I swear they exchanged a look."

"A look?" Evie didn't feel entirely convinced. "They might have been acknowledging each other. Obviously, they've seen each other around the hotel and the general area."

Caro straightened. "I also saw a nod. Yes, I'm certain I saw a nod. It felt like the type of nod one would employ to confirm something."

"That's more like it. What could they have been agreeing to?" Evie wondered.

"Well, Mr. Prentiss is still here so we can't assume it was a meeting place," Tom said.

"I wonder if they'd had a previous conversation." Evie looked over her shoulder. Mr. Prentiss hadn't moved. "Or they might be communicating through notes. I can imagine them exchanging messages outlining their plan, which Mr. Addington put into action by driving out to... wherever he went." Now they would have to wait until Edmonds returned. Evie checked her watch. "We crossed paths with Edmonds an hour ago. Did you warn him not to take any unnecessary risks?"

"Of course, milady. I would not send him off on a silly or a dangerous errand. He has instructions to keep his distance and report back."

Yes, but how far would Edmonds have to follow Mr. Addington? "Would Mr. Addington have taken that road if he is headed to London?" Evie asked.

Tom drew in a long breath and pushed it out slowly. "Yes."

"Just how committed do you think Edmonds will be to following him? Heavens, what if he does go all the way to London?"

"I trust Edmonds. He'll have better sense than to do that, milady." Caro bit her bottom lip. "At least, I hope he will. Yes, I'm sure he will."

Evie didn't want to say it, but she feared Edmonds might take the task to heart. "I suppose Mr. Addington wouldn't go very far. After all, his wife is still here. That is, I assume she is."

Caro nodded. "I only saw Mr. Addington leaving."

Evie finished her tea and decided now would be a good time to change out of her driving clothes. "I will see you both shortly. Hopefully, by then, there will be some good news."

Getting up she noticed a wave of people entering the hotel. The gentlemen headed toward the library, while the ladies made their way up the grand staircase at a leisurely pace.

Evie decided to take the back stairs to avoid being delayed by their leisurely pace. A second later, she felt a presence behind her. Without thinking, she turned and nearly collided with Tom.

"Are you following me?"

"I might be."

"Honestly, this is a hotel. Look around you. There are people everywhere."

"I'll just walk you to the stairs. Then, I'll double back and ask to use the manager's office. I'd like to call the tea room proprietress in Findon and ask if she happened to see a *Duesenberg* drive by."

"Oh, that's a fabulous idea, Tom. Great thinking. At least we'll know something."

They continued on their way toward the back of the hotel and the stairs. Reaching them, Evie turned and smiled. "This is where we part ways."

Tom peered up the stairs and nodded. "Be quick about it."

Sliding her hand along the balustrade, Evie hurried up the stairs. She reached the landing and looked down only to find Tom still standing at the foot of the stairs. "Would you like me to send smoke signals when I reach my room?"

"Just holler and slam the door shut. I'll hear you."

Rolling her eyes, she scurried up the rest of the way. Thinking it wouldn't hurt to play it safe, when she reached her floor, Evie slowed down and turned her attention to her surroundings.

Once inside her room, she made sure to lock the door behind her.

Without the benefit of Caro's assistance, Evie selected a light green skirt and white blouse matched with a lightweight coat the same color and length as the skirt. She stood staring at her hat boxes for long minutes. Evie knew Caro maintained a strict order. She made it look simple enough. Peering inside one hat box, she found the offensive cherry straw hat she had decided would never again see the light of day.

As she searched through the rest of the boxes looking for a suitable hat, she thought about their mode of transportation. Motor car travel had certainly freed them up, but there was a lot to be said for trains and their schedules.

If Mr. Addington had traveled by train, they would have a timetable to work with, as well as a possible destination. They might even establish that destination by visiting the train station and relying on the station master to remember a few pertinent details. With the freedom afforded by motor cars came the freedom of choice. One road could lead to another and another...

Dismissing her thoughts, Evie settled for a light orange cloche which more or less matched the light shade of green she wore. Adjusting the hat, she sat at the small desk opposite one of the windows.

Equipped with pen and paper, Evie set to work on a list.

"Mr. Prentiss visited Findon and approached May Fields." Had coincidence brought them together in Worthing? Tapping the pen on the desk, she said, "Mr. Addington. How are you connected?"

She made a note to contact her man of business only to cross it out. If Mr. Matthew Keys had discovered something new, he would have contacted Evie.

Had she asked him to also look into Mr. Addington?

Shaking her head, Evie wrote the name down again. She would telephone Mr. Matthew Keys to make sure...

Half an hour later, a knock at the door startled her. Caro walked in, followed by Tom.

"My apologies," Evie said, "I lost track of time."

Caro went straight to one of the hat boxes, retrieved a hat and replaced the one Evie had chosen.

A glance in the mirror made Evie smile. Yes, much better. Same shade of green but slightly lighter.

"I telephoned Mrs. Johnstone," Tom said. "She saw Edmonds drive by several times. Apparently, he is on his way back."

"Driving around?"

"Yes, he actually stopped at the tea room and asked if anyone had seen a *Rolls-Royce*."

"He lost Mr. Addington?"

Nodding, Tom said, "I suspect he lost him somewhere in Findon."

"At least we know he's safe. I worried something might have happened to Edmonds." Turning to Caro, she asked, "I take it Mr. Prentiss is no longer downstairs?"

"Mr. Prentiss went up to his room. That's why I abandoned my post."

"Oh, Caro. You don't need to stay on his trail. I believe my man of business will dig up something soon."

"I hope so because I'm beginning to lose hope. Milady, I'm afraid you got me all excited about getting justice for May Fields."

"It will happen, Caro. Don't you worry about it." Evie brightened. "I think the three of us should have lunch together."

"If you don't mind, I would rather stay behind and wait for Edmonds, milady. I'm sure he'll have a tale and a half to tell when he returns."

Standing in front of the mirror, Evie inspected her reflection. "Caro, you said Mr. Prentiss returned to his room. Where was Mrs. Prentiss? Did you see her go down?"

"Oh, I never thought to look for her."

"This is probably the first time both men have been in public without their respective partners," Evie observed.

"Perhaps she has come to her senses and left him," Tom suggested.

Evie looked confused enough for Tom to remind her of her earlier theory about Mr. Prentiss marrying his wife for her fortune.

"Money." Evie sat on the edge of the chaise longue. "We haven't actually discussed it."

"Do we need to?" Tom asked.

"We should consider it. Plenty of people are murdered for money."

Tom crossed his arms and rocked on his heels. "Do you think May Fields had money? And, if she did, how could Mr. Prentiss gain by her death?"

Evie's eyes widened. "What if that is the reason why Mr. Prentiss approached May Fields in the first place. He might have had news about an inheritance she had never expected. We've considered the idea of Mr. Prentiss working with someone else. What if another heir engaged him to get rid of May Fields so they could inherit?" Evie liked the idea so much, she wanted it to be true. However, she then remembered what Ruth Charles had said. Mr. Prentiss had actually offered May Fields a job. "Forget I said that." Surging to her feet, she groaned. "Oh, this waiting for Edmonds has put me on edge. I wish he'd hurry up with some news."

The sound of a hard thump had everyone stilling.

One by one, they looked up.

Evie thought she heard a door open and close again. Standing as they were in silence, they all became aware of the slightest sounds from a floorboard creaking to someone talking.

"Did it come from the room above?" Evie asked.

"Hard to say." Tom moved to the door and pressed his ear to it. After a moment, he opened the door a fraction. "I see a couple walking away from the room next door. Perhaps it was them."

How far did sound travel, Evie wondered. "Caro, where is your room?"

"The next floor up at the end of the hallway. It's a corner room."

When Evie didn't say anything, Caro suggested going up and walking around her room.

"Oh, that is a fabulous idea."

Tom and Evie waited in silence. Then they heard the sounds of firm footsteps and something hard hitting the floor.

"I guess sound travels in this building," Evie said.

"Did you hear that?" Tom asked. He strode to the window and peered out. "It sounded like someone saying hello."

Evie joined him by the window and pointed toward the corner of the building. "Wave. That's Caro on her balcony." Swinging away from the window, Evie remembered the concierge had told Tom all the windows were left open during the day to air out the rooms.

Had someone heard May Fields?

"Oh," Evie exclaimed. Stumbling back, she collided with the desk, swung away and collided with the chaise longue.

"What's wrong?"

"I just remembered something... I think I heard May Fields." Evie's legs wobbled.

She heard Tom rush toward her, felt his hands clasp her arms. Her ears buzzed and she swooned...

Heavens...

CHAPTER 16

*C*aro entered Evie's room saying, "I paced around my room, then I stomped about. Did you hear a thump? I dropped one of my cases on the floor." Closing the door, she turned and exclaimed, "Milady!" Caro rushed toward Evie. "What happened?"

Evie groaned and pressed her hand to her forehead. "Oh... Caro."

Tom crouched down beside Evie. "She sort of lost her balance."

"I think my mind froze. Or I suffered some sort of shock." Evie turned to Caro. "Do you remember the day we arrived, you came in and woke me up?"

"Yes, of course."

"I said something about being woken up."

"You did grumble a little."

"No, I didn't complain about being woken up by you." Evie brushed her hand across her brow. "Something else woke me up several times while I slept. I remember being in that sort of drowsy state between sleep and wakefulness."

"Oh, yes. You said you couldn't recommend the hotel for its peace and quiet."

"That's right. Excellent memory, Caro."

"Would you like a cup of tea?"

"Oh, no. No more tea, please. I think I need coffee. Yes, a strong cup of coffee will make me feel better."

"I'll take care of it," Tom said.

Evie straightened. Had she heard May Fields stumbling about in a drunken state? She groaned again.

"What?" Caro took hold of her hand.

"I think I might have heard the maid." She slumped back. "What if I could have prevented her death?"

"Milady, you mustn't think like that."

"Yes, but... If I'd gone up to complain about the noise, I might have been able to stop her. If, indeed, she threw herself off the balcony. Or, if my other theory is correct, I might have stopped the person who killed her first and then, hours later, pushed her off."

"Or, you might have been killed too. There is no point in wondering what might have happened. You will only burden yourself with guilt."

"You are being far too sensible, Caro. Please allow me to wallow in a moment of guilt. Something else might come to me." Evie clicked her fingers. "I remember the drive here left me thoroughly exhausted."

"Yes, I remember you declined to have anything for lunch and came straight up to your room. You wouldn't even let me unpack for you."

Had she seen anything out of the ordinary along the way, something she might not have thought of as curious at the time? Someone else making their way up the stairs or someone rushing down the stairs?

"I don't know what came over me. When I heard you stomping around your room, my mind must have made the connection and then I swooned. I don't swoon. I have never swooned."

"You have now. And... what does it all mean?" Caro asked.

"I don't know but this is going to keep me awake all night, I'm sure. The sounds I heard that first day were loud enough to wake me up... So, I have to assume they came from the room directly above mine. We know May Fields went back in there at precisely midday."

"You came to your room after that," Caro said.

"Yes! And I collapsed on the bed straightaway."

"I came to wake you up after two in the afternoon."

Evie closed her eyes for a moment and then said, "Assuming May Fields started drinking straightaway, she might have reached a state of inebriation within the hour." Evie looked up at the ceiling. "I heard loud thumps. I'm sure of it. I've never had more than a couple of glasses of wine so I have no real idea what happens when you drink too much."

Caro's cheeks brightened slightly.

"Caro, is there something you wish to share?"

"Well..." Caro grinned. "There was that one time at Christmas. My mother makes the best mulled wine and did I mention it was Christmas?"

Evie nodded. "A couple of times. I take it you drank more than you are accustomed to drinking."

"Yes. My legs wobbled and when I tried to get up, I swayed. I might have stumbled but my brother caught me in time."

Evie smiled. "That's what brothers are for. Are you suggesting May Fields might have been sitting down while drinking and then she rose to her feet and stumbled?"

"Precisely. Yes."

"If we are to believe she had been upset by Mr. Prentiss... for whatever reason, I suppose we could assume she drank herself into a stupor in a short time."

Caro paced around the room. "I'm trying to picture her being upset and swilling that brandy in greedy, self-pitying gulps."

Evie hummed under her breath. "Oh, yes. I'm picturing it now. However, it contradicts my theory of May Fields being pushed off the balcony."

"Does it? Someone might have found her closer to five in a full state of inebriation and taken advantage of it."

"Oh, yes." Evie clapped. "Yes. I like that theory. She would not have been able to put up a struggle. Oh, how I wish I had been in my room. I would have heard it all." Instead, she had been out and about having a jolly good time.

"Please tell me you are not about to have another attack of guilt."

Could she have done something to prevent May Fields' death? "Where is that coffee?" And why hadn't

Tom simply telephoned for it? Evie supposed he hadn't been entirely comfortable seeing her so upset.

The door opened and Tom strode in followed by a waiter carrying a tray.

Smiling, Tom said, "I heard you bellow for coffee."

"Yes, well, we have already established the fact. Sound travels in this hotel." She turned to Caro. "Do we have the same problem at Halton House?"

"I don't believe we do, milady."

"Perhaps the sea air has eroded the walls." Evie thanked the waiter and busied herself pouring a cup of coffee.

A knock at the door was interrupted when the waiter opened it to leave.

"Ah, Edmonds," Evie exclaimed. "Do come in." She called out to the waiter, "Could we please have some tea and some sandwiches brought up?"

"Milady, I'm sorry it took so long to return," Edmonds said.

"What news do you bring? We have been so eager to hear from you. At one point, we thought you might have driven all the way to London."

"Ah, yes. It nearly came to that. I had been keeping the *Rolls-Royce* in sight but then, as we neared the village of Findon, the *Rolls* slowed down so I had to match its speed. I must have taken my eyes off it for no longer than a second. In the next instant, the motor car had disappeared. I thought it might have gone along one of the side lanes. I tried one and then another. I must have driven around the village five times before I finally stopped and made inquiries at the tea room."

"Yes, we are aware of that." Evie smiled at Tom.

"As it turned out," Edmonds continued, "the proprietress noticed me driving by but not the *Rolls-Royce*. That led me to believe it must have driven along another road right before arriving at the village. So, I went investigating." Edmonds eyed the pot of coffee.

"Would you like some coffee?"

He took a deep swallow and nodded.

Evie waited for Edmonds to finish his drink before asking, "And what did you discover?"

"I caught sight of the back of the motor car protruding from a side lane. So I stopped and walked toward it. I peered around the corner and didn't see anyone in the motor car."

Evie looked up at Tom who stood near the window. "Mr. Addington must have gone to Findon to see someone." Turning to Edmonds, she asked, "Did you see yellow roses in the garden?" She hadn't noticed them on any of the other cottages except the one where Ruth Charles worked at.

Edmonds nodded. "Yes, there were yellow roses in the house next door."

Evie tried to recall something significant about the house, something that would set it apart from the others. Something other than a profusion of yellow roses. "Tom, did you notice anything about that house?"

He tapped his chin. "There was something hanging by the front door. Let me think…"

"Oh, the light. It reminded me of the lights that used to hang by the side of the old horse drawn coaches."

"Yes, that's it."

"Oh, yes." Edmonds nodded. "That's the house. I think…"

Tom and Evie reacted to the news in much the same way, both withdrawing into silence. How could they be sure Mr. Addington had gone to that house?

Tom shifted and then turned to look out of the window.

Evie folded her arms and tipped her chin down. She tossed around a few ideas and felt herself wince a couple of times at the absurdity of some of her thoughts. She even argued in favor of some of them. When she looked up, she saw both Caro and Edmonds watching her, their eyes slightly widened.

"Will you all think I am on the verge of lunacy if I suggest Mr. Addington went to visit Ruth Charles?"

"No," Tom answered without hesitating. "But why would he do that?"

"Heavens, it was puzzling enough when we made a forced connection between Mr. Prentiss and Mr. Addington. Now we have to add Ruth Charles to the plot that is already too thick for my liking. How am I ever going to convince the detective he needs to look into May Fields' death? We have no solid proof of anything. But we do have a lot of…" Evie clicked her fingers.

"Suspicions?" Tom suggested.

"Yes, and a lot of circumstances we can't explain." Evie glanced at Edmonds. She had wanted to ask him for details of what he had seen when May Fields had fallen… jumped or been pushed to her death, but the man looked exhausted.

Edmonds cleared his throat. "There is more…"

Evie shifted to the edge of her seat. "I'm sorry. We must have cut you off with our silent musings."

"After I saw the motor car, I returned and moved the *Duesenberg* to the next street up where it couldn't be spotted. Then I returned and waited in hiding."

Evie, Caro and Tom stared at Edmonds without blinking.

Evie couldn't help thinking about Tom's earlier remark about her curiosity and eagerness to delve into the mysterious death being contagious.

"I waited until the gentleman stepped out of the house. He hurried to his motor car and drove off. He came out of the house with the yellow roses."

It took a moment for Evie to realize they now had confirmation. Mr. Addington had visited Ruth Charles.

CHAPTER 17

"*D*etective Inspector O'Neill is not in his office. His secretary would not say when he would return." Evie huffed out a breath. "I am trying to take the right steps and inform the police of our findings and they are being dreadfully inconsiderate."

"Unless, of course, the esteemed detective is out and about, actually doing his job and hunting down a criminal," Tom suggested.

"Yes, well... His timing could not be worse. What are we supposed to do with this information? If I don't tell someone of authority about it, I fear my head will explode." Evie scowled at the telephone. The person who had answered hadn't even asked if Evie wished to leave a message.

Rising to his feet, Tom walked to the door and held it open for her.

Evie gave him a half-hearted smile. "I have no idea what the manager must be thinking about us needing to use his office with so much frequency."

"You needn't worry about that. I told him you are in the midst of a dilemma that threatens to ruin your stay at the hotel and you wish to sort it out as soon as possible."

"I can only say I am blessed to have you, Caro and Edmonds with me. You are all watching my back and also making sure I don't trip over my own feet."

Tom checked his watch. "It's too late even for a late luncheon. Would you care for a stroll and some afternoon tea?"

"Yes, a breath of fresh air will do me a world of good. I can't think of anything better than to walk off my frustration."

Exiting the hotel manager's office, Evie surged ahead and walked at a brisk pace. As she rounded the corner leading to the lobby she collided with a woman. Evie gasped. "I am so sorry. How clumsy of me."

The other woman muttered an apology, straightened and hurried away.

Tom took Evie's elbow and guided her toward the exit. Halfway along the lobby, they both turned and saw the woman disappearing into the library.

"Tom, would I be imposing on you if I ask you to go see if she is meeting someone in the library? I have a feeling that might have been Mrs. Addington."

"Wait here for me."

Evie moved away from the door and went to stand near a window. She could see a few puffy clouds hovering in the distance but the day remained bright and sunny. Caro and Edmonds had been only too happy to step out and make the best of what remained of the afternoon.

She was about to look back toward the library when she noticed a familiar motor car parked outside the hotel.

The *Rolls-Royce* they had seen Mr. Addington driving.

It had to be the same one…

Tom returned and guided her outside. "The woman you bumped into was Mrs. Addington and she went into the library to meet Mr. Addington."

So… He had returned to the hotel. Evie pointed at the motor car. "Do you think that's his *Rolls*?"

"Most likely."

"I suppose they looked as cheerful as ever."

"Yes, they did." Tom pushed out a hard breath. "Now I find myself trying to decipher the way they looked but I'm afraid my skills might not be as good as Caro's observation skills. Her interpretation of the look she saw exchanged between Mr. Prentiss and Mr. Addington yielded positive results."

"Yes, positive but also perplexing," Evie said. "What would a detective do with this information? The two men are staying at the same hotel. We haven't seen them together and yet, during a brief encounter, they exchange a look that is enough to trigger Caro's suspicions. Eventually, we are led to the discovery of another participant in this mystery." Evie didn't wait for Tom to answer. "I think a detective would haul Ruth Charles into the station and subject her to a severe line of questioning."

Evie fumed in silence. She had reached a point of feeling quite helpless. Scooping in a breath, she tried to clear her mind. "I suppose I should look around for some sort of memento to take back with me, some sort of proof I have been on vacation." She drew in another breath only to gasp. "Heavens, what if Mr. Addington made a trip to Findon merely to express his condolences? I know it's unlike me to find sympathy for one of my targets, but it is quite possible he meant to do nothing more than... well, what I did. If I think about it, we went to Findon for that very reason."

"Are you feeling better now?" Tom asked.

Evie lifted her chin. "No, I believe I am trying to distract myself from being cross with Detective Inspector O'Neill. I'm sure he is doing his best to avoid me. I'm almost tempted to pay the local constabulary a visit but the prospect of another encounter with that dreadful man is enough to put me off the idea. Don't you dare suggest we stop somewhere for a cup of tea. I am still burdened by a great deal of unnecessary frustration."

Tom looked around. "I wonder if there is a shooting gallery somewhere. It might do you a world of good to vent some of that frustration on a target. Or perhaps we could visit the library."

Evie pointed over her shoulder. "I'm sure the library is in the opposite direction."

"So it is."

"Actually, where are we going?" Looking around, she saw some people strolling along in the same direction but most were headed the other way, toward the pier.

"I've had a couple of brief conversations with the concierge," Tom said. "He tells me there have been many people of note staying or living in the area. Among them, the Chief Magistrate of the Bow Street office and head of the Bow Street Runners."

"Bow Street Runners?" Evie had heard of them. She searched her memory and remembered seeing mention of them in a story she'd read.

"Yes, it was London's first official police force back in the 1800s. I believe they disbanded in 1839. Anyhow, Sir Frederick Adair Roe settled in the area and lived in what is referred to as the Beach House. Mention of the name reminded me of something. Or, rather, someone."

"Are we headed there now?"

"If I tell you, then that will spoil the surprise."

Evie smiled. "I'll try to remember to act surprised."

"As I was saying, mention of the house triggered a memory. It finally came to me. The current owner is a playwright."

"Oh, Phillipa would have loved that. She will not stop berating herself for turning down the invitation to join us. I will simply have to remind her of her priorities." Evie stopped. "Wait a minute. How do you know he's a playwright?"

Tom sighed. "It's rather a long story."

"Are we going to meet him?"

"No."

"Oh. This is your attempt to distract me. We are going there to admire the architecture."

"You can do that, if you like. The owner is currently traveling but he has given permission for us to visit."

"Heavens. How did that happen? When did you organize it?" Evie glanced at Tom and saw him staring into the distance. "Is this one of your secrets?"

"Not as such. I suppose you could say I have some connections. People who know people."

"That sounds rather vague."

"You're right. I made the arrangements as a possible distraction. As for how I know him. Actually, I met him in London, at a bar."

"Did you happen to be waiting for me?"

"I think so. I don't recall exactly. You might have been at a dress fitting."

"And you were killing time at a bar?"

Tom nodded. "He'd been visiting his sister in London. She's a sculptress. Anyhow, we talked for over an hour and then he mentioned being a playwright. At the time, he was working on an adaptation of The Three Musketeers. Long story short, I have spent some of my recent waiting time productively."

"Waiting time? Oh, you mean… Your pacing in the lobby while waiting for me to be ready time."

"Yes, that's it. I'm looking forward to seeing the house. Edward Knoblock…"

"Who is he?"

"He's the playwright I mentioned. He purchased the house in 1917. I am told King Edward VII stayed at the house several times while visiting the previous owner, Sir Edmund Loder and his family."

"Oh, I wish you'd mentioned this before. We could have asked Caro and Edmonds to join us."

They steered away from the main street running alongside the beach and headed down a side street.

"The house actually faces the beach, but the main entrance is on the other side," Tom explained.

Evie pointed ahead. "Oh, is that Caro and Edmonds? Yes, they're waving."

Tom smiled.

"Wait a minute. *Wait a minute.* Did you ask them to meet us here?"

"I might have."

"What else do you have up your sleeves?" Evie asked.

"I guess you'll just have to wait to find out."

"It seems I am the only one being kept in the dark. Look. Caro and Edmonds are walking off. That means they know where you are headed and are going to beat us to the house. I feel rather left out. What else have you planned for me?"

"If I tell you, it won't be a surprise."

"For your information, I have just come to realize I do not like surprises."

Tom laughed. "That's because you like to be in charge."

"I'm not sure how I feel about that observation." After a moment, she said, "You think my frustration stems from the fact I haven't been able to wield any control over the detective."

"I could not have expressed it better myself."

The impressive white building stood in the middle of a large park which extended all the way to the sea. Caro and Edmonds stood outside admiring the house.

"Did Tom tell you about his surprise?" Caro asked.

"No, he is making me wait."

The front door opened even before they reached it. Had they been expected?

"Good afternoon, Mr. Winchester."

The butler knew Tom?

"Good afternoon, Richards. Has he arrived?"

"He has indeed. This way, please."

They followed the butler through to a sitting room beautifully furnished with pieces from a previous era. It seemed the owner was quite a collector of Regency furniture.

"Lady Woodridge."

Evie swung toward the familiar voice. Her mouth gaped open. Such was her surprise, she couldn't bring herself to speak.

She looked at Tom who exclaimed, "Surprise!"

Finally, Evie managed to say, "Detective."

Detective Inspector O'Neill looked rather pleased with himself. He shook hands with Tom and Edmonds and gave Caro a nod of acknowledgment.

"Well, now that I'm here, would you care to fill me in on everything that has been happening?"

CHAPTER 18

"I'm still not over the surprise of finding you here," Evie said. "When did this happen? How?"

Everyone turned to Tom who gave a casual shrug. "The reason the detective couldn't take your call was because he'd been making his way here. I telephoned him yesterday and explained the situation."

Evie pressed her hands to her cheeks. "And now you are here to solve the murder."

The detective nodded. "I am only here to look into it. You must understand, I find myself in a rather difficult situation. I cannot be seen to be treading on anyone's toes."

"You won't be," Evie said. "The local police are not interested in investigating May Fields' death."

"It's quite possible they missed something."

Evie gave an unladylike snort. "As it is, we have made three connections which cannot be explained and we have several theories, which I believe are worth looking into."

"Tell me what happened from the beginning," Detective O'Neill invited. "It will help me understand something about the initial police response. That is usually when they decide if there is a case or not."

"It might actually help us to know what you know first," Evie said.

Agreeing, the detective filled her in. He had spoken with his colleague at length. According to the local detective, his officers had failed to detect any sign of foul play. When Detective O'Neill went on to explain the next steps in any investigation, Evie shook her head.

"I didn't see any preservation of evidence. The guests remained in the same room. If there had been proof of a struggle it will all be gone now. The room has been cleaned every day since the incident took place."

"I would still like to hear your full version of the events as you saw them, my lady."

Evie accepted a cup of tea from the butler and took a quick sip before telling the detective about all the theories they had been entertaining.

"Sound theorizing is essential to any investigation," he said, "but you, my dear Countess, have taken it one step further. I can see why you didn't take your information to the local police. It all sounds fictional."

Evie wanted to protest, but Detective O'Neill had a point. "What about Mr. Addington's visit to Ruth Charles?"

"You said it yourself, my lady. Mr. Addington might have been expressing his condolences. You found out about Ruth Charles because you made a point of following up on your need to express your condolences. It's quite possible Mr. Addington did the same."

Again, Evie wanted to protest, but the detective held up his hand. "However, I am interested in what your maid, Caro, saw. Have you heard more from your man of business?"

Evie shook her head. "I expect he will contact me soon. He said he wanted to be thorough."

The detective looked out of the window. "This is a magnificent view."

Thinking everyone needed a break from her, Evie took the opportunity to look around the room. Her attention settled on a painting above the fireplace of a man in military uniform. She turned to Tom. "Is that the scriptwriter?"

"Yes."

"You didn't tell me he had served in the war."

"Yes, he joined up right after he became a British citizen."

"Oh?"

"He was actually born in New York."

Evie turned to the painting again. A while back, Tom had come up with a story about meeting a Duke at the Battle of the Somme. Evie knew there was more truth than fiction to his story because Tom had served in the Great War... "You said you met him at a bar but I'm guessing you knew him well before that encounter."

"I guess so."

The detective finished his tea and set his cup down. "Your man of business appears to have led you to make the first connection."

"Yes, he found out Mr. Prentiss had visited Findon. Tom and I took it from there and discovered Mr. Prentiss had spoken with May Fields. It is far too coincidental for her to then use his balcony to jump to her death."

"I agree."

"You do?" A wave of relief swept through Evie. "So, where do we go from here?"

"Ordinarily, the police would work out a strategy and collect information about everyone involved. You appear to have singled out a couple of people."

"Three if we count Ruth Charles. I'm willing to bet she is somehow involved. As we have only now learned of Mr. Addington's visit to Findon, I have not had the time to come up with a story. However, I am prepared to suspend any idea of Mr. Addington visiting her to offer his condolences. The fact he and Mr. Prentiss exchanged a look that struck Caro as being one of agreement, means there is something peculiar happening."

"The Countess has a few theories on the matter," Tom said.

The detective brushed a hand across his chin. "It might be a good idea to work out some sort of timeline and place everyone you think is involved."

Evie produced a small leather-bound notebook. "I have already noted down a few names."

The detective looked around. "We could do with a flat surface. It would help to have all the information in one place."

The butler cleared his throat. "I have been instructed to provide you with everything you might need, including the use of the house."

Everyone expressed their surprise and appreciation.

"Perfect. That means we won't have to sneak around or meet in my room." Turning to the detective, Evie asked, "Does this mean you will stay on and investigate the matter?"

"In an unofficial capacity. Yes. After all, Tom has gone to some trouble to organize accommodation for me."

"Oh, where will you be staying?"

"Right here, I believe."

The butler nodded.

Just how well did Tom know the owner of the house?

A footman appeared and assisted the butler in clearing a table.

They spent the next hour going through everything they had put together while the detective took notes, spreading some pages out on the table.

"I think it might be a good idea to contact your man of business and tell him to direct his telephone calls here," Tom suggested.

"Yes," Evie agreed. "That will be a relief. I'm sure the hotel manager is beginning to suspect we are really up to no good. Also, I haven't actually stopped suspecting the hotel manager or the owner. They would both benefit if the police didn't look into this death and dismissed it as an accident."

She watched the detective studying the notes he'd taken. He tapped one of the pieces of paper. "You say Edmonds saw the victim fall to her death."

"Oh, yes," Evie exclaimed. "In fact, I've been meaning to ask him a few questions about that." She saw Caro nudging Edmonds to attention. "Edmonds, I'm sorry if this upsets you, but can you describe exactly what you saw?"

When he finished, Evie shivered. She would hate to have to live with the memory. "Again, I'm sorry to ask, but… did she flail her arms? It seems to me that's just what I would do if I fell by accident. In fact, that is precisely what I did once. Back home, we have a lake with trees close to the shoreline. I had clambered onto an overhanging branch because I wanted to dangle my feet over the water. I lost my balance and fell in. I recall that moment when I tried to grab hold of a branch. My arms flailed about. In the end, I fell in."

They all turned toward Edmonds. After a moment, he shook his head.

"I didn't see her arms move."

"At all?" the detective asked.

Again, Edmonds gave it some thought. "Her arms almost looked stiff."

The detective's eyebrows curved up.

Evie thought she heard him murmur something. "Did you say rigor mortis?"

He nodded. "It usually sets in two to six hours after a person dies."

Evie shifted and looked from Tom to the detective. "Are you suggesting she might have already been dead when she fell from the balcony?"

The detective gave a small, noncommittal nod.

Evie surged to her feet and strode around the sitting room. Stopping by the fireplace, she tapped her finger against her chin.

"Milady," Caro said. "Remember what we talked about earlier?"

Evie sighed. "Yes." Did she dare share the information with the detective? Deciding she had nothing to lose, she said, "I heard noises. They were loud enough to wake me up." She filled in the details and then strode back to her chair and sat down.

"Are you suggesting she might have been killed at around midday?" the detective asked.

"Possibly closer to one in the afternoon. I'm sure I fell into a deep sleep straightaway. I'm guessing the noises stirred me awake between one and two in the afternoon. When Caro woke me up at two, I felt as if I hadn't slept at all."

The detective stepped away from the table and turned to look at the sea. "She fell to her death at five."

"Someone might have thrown her over the balcony," Evie suggested. "We have been having the most dreadful time trying to figure out what happened between the time May Fields went into Mr. Prentiss' room to replace the soap and the time she died, several hours later. I am convinced she did not come out of the room. Caro has spoken with all the staff working at the hotel and no one saw her after midday. Of course, we have to assume they are all innocent." Evie sighed. She had given little thought to anyone else being involved. "I seem to have become fixated with pointing the finger of suspicion at Mr. Prentiss and, now, Mr. Addington."

The detective brushed his fingers along his chin in such a manner, Evie assumed he had, at one time, sported a beard.

"Motive." Turning, he looked at Evie. "I believe you were right to focus on Mr. Prentiss. After all, the death took place in his room. Then, there is the information discovered by your man of business which led you to visit Findon where you learned of Mr. Prentiss' interest in May Fields. Somehow, we must discover the precise time he left the tea room and returned to the hotel. Someone is bound to have seen him."

"We know he left the tea room at four forty-five." Evie explained to the detective how they had come by that information. She turned to Caro. "Did you ask around the tea rooms and premises in the immediate area?"

"I did, milady. No one remembers the couple and he did not present his card anywhere else."

"Tom and I believe that had been Mr. Prentiss' way of establishing his whereabouts in case anyone questioned him. I keep saying that because I believe it is one of the most significant discoveries we have come up with. As to what time he returned to the hotel... The afternoons are quite busy. Most guests tend to return at about five in the afternoon to prepare for the evening. Some of them linger downstairs." Evie looked at Tom. "Others use the library or the bar. We only know what time he left the tea room. We have no idea if he went straight to his room or if he lingered down-stairs." Or, she thought, they might both have gone upstairs, seen May Fields and... pushed her off the balcony. Evie shook her head and revisited the latest theory.

Tom cleared his throat. "We have been playing around with the idea Mr. Prentiss killed May Fields before leaving the hotel and then threw her over the balcony when he returned to the hotel."

Evie surged to her feet. "We need to place him at the hotel just after five in the afternoon." Evie clicked her fingers. "He kills May Fields at midday. Goes out with his wife for afternoon tea. Returns to the hotel..." She swung away and paced about the room. "Since he went to the trouble of placing himself at the front desk when he left and at the tea room shortly before leaving, he would have taken great care to avoid being seen going up the stairs. If he did go up, we would need to find a reliable witness, otherwise, how will we know he returned to his room to do the deed?"

"Locard's principle," the detective said. "Every contact leaves a trace."

Evie and Tom exchanged a puzzled look.

The detective went on to explain, "Locard's prin-ciple holds that the perpetrator of a crime will bring something into the crime scene and leave with some-thing from it."

"Finding something that will incriminate Mr. Pren-tiss will be problematic, inspector. The crime took place in his room. The bottle is likely to have his fingerprints on it. Assuming, that is, that the empty bottle hasn't been disposed of. Either the police took it as evidence or they dismissed it as inconsequential." Evie crossed her arms and tapped her foot. "Tell me more about that principle."

Brushing his hand across his chin, the detective said, "Everything the perpetrator does bears mute witness against him. Where he steps, whatever he touches, whatever he leaves or takes with him… Physical evidence carries greater weight than the word of witnesses."

"I assume you are trying to make a point," Evie said, "by, understandably, explaining police procedures because you don't wish to undermine your colleague's efforts. You are to be commended for your loyalty. Let's say the local police did everything according to the book and actually found no reason to open an investigation. Do you believe there is reason to suspect foul play even without physical proof?"

He did not answer straightaway. In fact, he appeared to be unwilling to commit to anything.

Evie added, "I understand this must be difficult for you."

"I will have to proceed with care." He straightened. "But I will look into it, in an unofficial capacity."

"Where do we go from here?" Evie asked.

"I would like to know more about Mr. Prentiss and Mr. Addington. If we can connect the two gentlemen, we might be able to confirm one of your theories."

"The one about them plotting together?"

He nodded.

"But what if my man of business isn't able to find anything else of value?"

"We'll deal with that problem when we come to it."

"Couldn't we just set a trap for them?" Caro asked.

They all turned toward Caro, their expressions surprised.

Caro's cheeks colored. "I mean… We could slip a note under their door asking why they killed May Fields."

"That is a genius idea, Caro."

CHAPTER 19

"*L*et's not be so hasty." The detective pointed at his notes on the table. "I would prefer to sift through what we have and then we can set something into motion."

Tom cleared his throat. "If it comes to that, I will insist on the Countess staying right out of it. In fact, it would be better if we all moved out of the hotel."

Evie's eyes widened. "You will rob me of the experience?"

"I would rather deal with your backlash than your grandmother's wrath."

"In that case, be prepared for my cold shoulder." Evie lifted her chin and turned to the detective. "Detective. You said physical evidence carries tremendous weight. What sort of physical evidence would the police look for in the scene of a crime?"

"Fibers," he said, his tone pensive. "Hair. Fingerprints."

"If there had been a struggle, there might be hair

fibers on his clothes," Evie suggested. "Someone will need to go into his room and inspect his wardrobe."

"Since we don't know if the hotel manager is clear of suspicion," the detective explained, "it would be difficult for me to request access to the room without alerting him. Also, keep in mind, I am here in an unofficial capacity."

"I could ask one of the maids," Caro piped in.

Tom and the detective exchanged a look that spoke of concern.

Evie nodded. "I know. I know. You both want to wait for my man of business to come through with more information. In any case, do we even know what May Fields looked like? If Caro finds a stray hair on Mr. Prentiss' coat, how will we know if it belonged to May Fields?" She turned toward Tom. "Oh, I just remembered. We saw a photograph of her. I think she might have had brown hair. But then, so does his wife."

Caro sighed. "I doubt we could even rely on length since, nowadays, we all have short hair."

"Who identified the body? That's something we haven't considered." Evie wondered if anyone would have been able to make a positive identification. After all, she had fallen face down.

The detective looked down at his shoes.

"Is there something you know?" Evie asked.

When he hesitated, Evie encouraged him. "I think we can bear to hear a few gory details."

"According to my colleague, the fall caused significant damage to her face. She was identified by her clothing."

"If I may be permitted to employ my imagination…"
Evie found a chair and sat down. "What if someone
caused the damage before she fell? Tom and I discussed
this but we were only filling in the time. As I recall, we
had run out of conversation."

Tom lifted his eyebrow as if surprised.

The detective held up a finger but he remained
silent. He turned toward the table and studied the
notes he'd made. "We would need to look for a weapon
in the room."

"Meaning, someone needs to go inside Mr. Prentiss'
room." Evie glanced at Caro. She wouldn't feel
comfortable sending her maid to snoop around.
"Surely the killer would have disposed of a weapon."
Evie closed her eyes. "I'm trying to picture my room.
I'm sure they are all alike. There's a lamp on the writing
desk. I'm guessing it's made of brass, which is quite
sensible as the desk sits against a window. There's also
a small statue on a side table. Oh, and the table lamp by
the bed. I'm sure that is also made of brass." Evie
clicked her fingers. "The weapon might be in plain
sight. The killer might have cleaned it, but as Detective
O'Neill pointed out, according to Locard's principle,
the perpetrator will have left some evidence behind."

Caro took a step forward. "I am quite willing to take
a look around. Edmonds can be my lookout."

Evie glanced at her watch. "It would be too risky
now. We'll need to wait until tomorrow morning when
the maids go into the rooms to clean. In any case, I'm
not entirely comfortable with you going in there
alone."

Caro looked at Edmonds and then at Tom. "Someone could dress as a waiter. I've become quite friendly with the maid. I'm sure she'll help us to gain access to the room."

The detective put his hands up. "Let's go through everything we know first."

"That won't take long." While the detective summarized everything Evie had told him, she strolled around the sitting room, taking her time to admire the various pieces on display.

To her surprise, the detective had even taken note of their most outrageous theories.

He checked his watch. "Perhaps we could use this time to discuss anything that comes to mind. Does anyone have any questions?"

Evie raised her hand. "What could drive a person to commit such a heinous crime?"

Tapping the table, the detective said, "The killer had something to lose." He sifted through the pieces of paper. "Here. You came up with the idea." He plucked a note from the table and held it up. "The maid overheard something."

"So, Mr. Prentiss and Mr. Addington decided they needed to get rid of the maid. They came up with a plan and... Oh, this means the killer did not act on impulse."

"That's right." The detective nodded. "He planned every detail, including the disposal of the body to make it look like an accident or an act of suicide."

As relieved as Evie felt by the inspector's presence, she couldn't shake off the edginess she sensed as well as the sense of urgency. If they didn't find solid proof, the killer would get away. "What is the process... or should that be procedure regarding the body? Is there a post mortem performed?"

"There wouldn't be in this case because the police have not found any sign of foul play," he said.

Evie gritted her back teeth together. "If I am correct and there was some sort of struggle..." She growled softly. "Give me a moment. I am trying to put myself in the place of the victim. What would I do? Punch. Claw. Scratch. I would definitely yell. I heard something but it sounded muffled. Perhaps the killer clamped his hand over her mouth."

"Has anyone had a close look at Mr. Prentiss?" the detective asked. "Did anyone notice any fresh scars or scratches on his face, his neck or his hands?"

"Tom and I have spent a great deal of time glancing at him. I can't say that I have noticed anything out of the ordinary. Then again, I hadn't been looking for anything specific."

Caro inspected her nails. "If she had tried to scratch her way out of the situation, it's possible there might be broken fingernails."

"Yes," the detective exclaimed and gave a firm nod. "We will need to look at the body." He brushed his hand across his face. "But it's not going to be easy. I will have to make a few telephone calls and see if I can find a contact, someone who can gain access to the body without looking suspicious."

The butler nodded. "You may use the telephone in the library."

The detective followed Richards out of the sitting room, leaving everyone else to ponder their situation in silence.

Seeing Caro standing by the window gazing out to sea, Evie suggested she and Edmonds might want to go out for a stroll around the grounds. "There's no point in you staying indoors. If anything happens, we'll call you."

The butler brought a fresh pot of coffee and informed them dinner was in the process of being prepared.

"That is wonderfully accommodating of you. Thank you."

"You are very welcome, my lady. Mr. Knoblock has been away for over a month now and the house has been too quiet."

Tom declined the offer of coffee so Evie poured herself a cup. "What do you make of all this, Tom?"

He sat down on a chair upholstered in turquoise with gold trimmings. "The detective finds himself in an awkward position but I'm sure he'll find a way around it." He looked pensive for a moment and then added, "I'm actually concerned about the failure to perform a post mortem. I know you have been annoyed with the lack of action from the police, but the omission to perform an autopsy makes their lack of action quite blatant. Almost deliberate. Thanks to Edmonds' observations, as well as your conclusion, we now suspect May Fields had already been dead when she fell off the balcony. Surely, the fact her body had already entered rigor mortis should have come to the attention of the police. It should have been spotted straightaway."

"Yes. Absolutely. Do you think Detective O'Neill is aware of the fact?"

"I fear he might be trying to avoid tackling the subject. It must be difficult for a policeman to suspect a fellow officer of negligence or, worse, some sort of wrongdoing or even collusion. Remember, you have also suspected the police of being somehow involved in a cover-up."

"Yes, well... I only said that because I was still cross with the local detective."

Tom leaned back and closed his eyes. "Picture it. A new hotel is opened. Disaster strikes. Someone dies. The hotel owner wants to avoid bad publicity. What would it take to make this problem go away?"

Bribery and corruption, Evie thought. "The detective will not like your theory, Tom."

"No, but he'll eventually come to realize there might be some truth to the story. Either that, or the local police is quite incompetent or guilty of overlooking the circumstances of a death because the victim was a mere maid."

"For his sake," Evie said, "I hope the local detective turns out to be incompetent. Overlooking details such as rigor mortis setting in on someone who has presumably only just jumped to her death won't look as bad as him taking a bribe for keeping everything quiet."

The door to the sitting room opened and the detective walked in, his manner preoccupied.

"Detective? Are you about to deliver bad news?"

He looked up. "Yes, I'm afraid so, my lady." He shook his head and raked his fingers through his hair. "The mortuary needed the extra room. As there had not been a case opened, they decided to go ahead with a cremation."

Evie gaped. "Impossible."

"I'm afraid it's all too true."

"But who gave the permission? I mean… I gave the detective my card. I told him I would take care of the arrangements…"

"He didn't see the need to impose on your generosity. Also, a close friend of the victim contacted him to collect May Fields' possessions and showed him a written statement signed by the victim stating she wished to be cremated because she didn't have any relatives who would visit a grave."

"A statement? I suppose the person who delivered this message was none other than Ruth Charles."

"I believe so. Yes."

Evie swung toward Tom. "Do you think that is the reason why Mr. Addington visited Ruth Charles?"

"It would seem like it."

Evie rubbed her fingers along her temple. "I'm going to telephone my man of business and tell him to place all calls to this number."

Cremated.

Even with her limited knowledge of police procedures, she knew the body could have revealed secrets…

Had it been cremated on purpose?

CHAPTER 20

"This salmon mousse is exquisite, Richards."

"Thank you, my lady. I shall pass on the compliments to the chef."

Everyone else had also offered their appreciation of the meal and had then fallen silent.

The thought of someone inspecting the body for clues had given Evie hope. And now those hopes had been dashed. So far, they hadn't been able to make any real progress and now they faced more uncertainties than they had before.

The detective spoke about his desire to spend a vacation fishing. He shared his enthusiasm with Edmonds who originally hailed from a small fishing village. This intrigued Caro because, before coming to Worthing, she had never once set foot on a beach.

"I should like to walk barefoot along the sand," Caro declared.

"I think I might join you, Caro. And then I might

build a sand castle. I will at least return home with some quaint stories to tell."

"You will have to have some stories at hand even if you don't walk barefoot on the sand," Tom said. "Unless, of course, you plan on sharing all this with the dowager."

"She's bound to have heard about it all by now." Evie had no trouble picturing Henrietta shaking her head in amusement and concern.

Evie had felt dismayed by the news of May Fields' body being cremated. Then, after her telephone conversation with her man of business, Mr. Matthew Keys, Evie had fallen into a state of despondency. Despite spending the entire day trying to find a connection between Mr. Prentiss and Mr. Addington, he hadn't been able to convey any new information. The private clubs the gentlemen in question frequented had not been easy to infiltrate. But he remained hopeful.

"I've been thinking," Caro said. "Instead of slipping a note under Mr. Prentiss' door, we could send a note to Ruth Charles saying something to prompt her, or rather, taunt her into taking action."

Evie lowered her fork. "You have our full attention, Caro."

"Well, if she is somehow involved, and I don't actually see how or why she would be, after all, she is supposed to be May Fields' best friend, I think she might go running to warn the people she is scheming with. Or she might try to make a run for it." Caro took a deep swallow. "Thereby implicating herself."

They all murmured in agreement.

"Also, I've been thinking about the body being cremated. If we are to assume the killer wanted to get rid of the evidence... What would May Fields' body have revealed? I suppose it's not a suitable subject for the dinner table. My apologies, milady."

"No need to apologize, Caro. We are all rather obsessed with the subject and eager to get to the bottom of it all." Evie savored some more of the salmon mousse and tried to focus on appreciating it.

She turned to the detective. "If the body is no longer available to reveal its secrets, can the room where she died be scrutinized. I know we have considered the possibility of looking for fibers or hair, but that is no longer an option as we have nothing to compare them to, even if anything is found. Is it possible the room itself might yield other information?"

The detective took a sip of his wine. Setting the glass down, he said, "In 1869, a French detective named *Gustave Macé* worked a case where he struggled to find traces of blood in a room where he knew a victim had died a brutal death. He had the bright idea of pouring water on the floor tiles. When the tiles were removed, the under-surface was found to be caked with blood. This led to a confession from the prime suspect. So, in answer to your question, yes. If we consider your theory about the victim being killed before being thrown off the balcony, there would be reason to believe the killer used something in the room as a weapon to commit the murder. A careful inspection of table lamps or statues could provide a valuable lead. It would definitely give us a starting point."

Meaning, he would have enough proof to demand the local police open an investigation.

"Perhaps we're thinking too much about the details," Evie said.

"What do you mean?" Caro asked.

What did she mean? Evie took a moment to think through her statement. It had simply occurred to her, surfacing from a mind muddled with facts and suppositions.

"Well, with the body gone, there is simply no way to know for sure if that was May Fields." Again, she stopped and mulled over the statement. It seemed so simple. All along, they had accepted the fact the person who had fallen or been thrown to her death was May Fields. "We have been assuming it was the maid because that's what we were told." She didn't want to say it out loud, but the local police had come under suspicion. Their negligence put everything they did or said into question. She turned to Tom. "Remember my surprise when you said the police had already spoken with the staff working at the hotel and would not be questioning the guests? I still maintain the police were rather swift in declaring it was the maid."

Everyone set their forks down and stared at Evie.

"Did I say something wrong?" Evie asked.

"I think this is the first time Edmonds has sat with the

gentlemen to drink port and smoke cigars," Caro observed as she stirred some sugar into her coffee.

Evie gave a pensive nod. "They were all so surprised by my remark, I expected them to forego the tradition."

"I'm sure they wished to spend some time in private praising you."

"Are you teasing me, Caro?"

"Not at all, milady. Men don't always enjoy admitting a woman can match their wits."

"True. But, surely, they would know by now. I am quite witty." Evie grinned. "Look at me, now I'm teasing myself."

Caro leaned forward and inspected the cakes displayed on a dainty platter. "If the victim was not May Fields, who could it be?"

Evie rose to her feet and strode over to the table to examine the notes the detective had made. "To think, we might already have observed the truth without even knowing it."

"Pardon?"

Evie shrugged. "Oh, you know the saying, it's right under your nose. What if the truth has been staring us in the face all along, only we were too distracted to notice?"

"Oh, I see," Caro said. "We should be able to access the room while the Prentiss couple is out and about. If there's some sort of evidence in there, I'm sure we'll find it. I mean… we suspect they cremated the body to hide the truth. Well, they can't possibly burn down the hotel to cover all their tracks…"

"Heavens. I do hope it doesn't come to that." They would have to take care. If the killer still resided in the hotel, he might be on the lookout. In fact, he might already have noticed someone making inquiries. Evie tipped her head back and imagined the waiter they'd spoken with at the tea room remarking to Mr. Prentiss about the couple who had been asking questions... "I'm now thinking it might be safer for us to end our stay at the hotel."

"But wouldn't that raise suspicions?" Caro asked. "The hotel management knows you are there for the week and we still haven't crossed them off the list of suspects."

Evie went to stand by the window. The sunny day had ended. The sun had set. Not that she'd had time to enjoy it or appreciate it. "It might force the killer to take action and, possibly, make a mistake. Our main suspects, Mr. Prentiss and Mr. Addington, have been going about their business. They have set a routine. We need to do something to prompt them into taking action."

The door to the sitting room opened, the butler walked in, followed by the others.

Exchanging a look of mutual understanding with Caro, Evie murmured, "This should be interesting."

The detective drew in a breath and smiled at Evie. "Lady Woodridge."

Oh, heavens.

"In all my years working as a detective, I have tried to maintain an open mind and, on occasion, suspend my disbelief. After all, in my line of work, we tend to rely on physical evidence but that doesn't always provide results."

"Heavens! I feel I am about to be reprimanded."

"On the contrary, my lady. I am trying to lead up to my praise. You have displayed a unique way of looking at things."

Evie smiled. "Oh, thank you. I hope it serves well."

"I believe so. Yes, indeed. I have taken the liberty of contacting a colleague. He will be making his way to Findon and keeping an eye on Miss Ruth Charles. The fact the victim has been cremated at her request suggests a possible awareness of the risks involved. The killer might suspect someone is taking an interest in the incident and is, as we speak, trying to cover his tracks."

"I take it you have used your cigar and port time to discuss my suggestion," Evie said.

"Oh, yes. Yes, indeed, we have. Tomorrow morning, we will organize ourselves for the first task at hand. If Caro is willing…" the detective looked at Caro who promptly nodded. "Then, as she suggested, she could make contact with the maid in charge of cleaning Mr. Prentiss' room and gain access. Edmonds will accompany her. I suggest using a damp white handkerchief to sweep through the solid objects which might have been used as a weapon."

Caro gave a firm nod. "I will be as thorough as if I were cleaning her ladyship's room. Not everyone knows this, but I actually started out as a maid." She looked at the detective. "I take it I will be looking for blood."

"Yes. Even the minutest amount might provide proof May Fields died in that room. Also, take a close look at the floors. There might be scuffle marks." Looking about the room, he added, "We shouldn't get our hopes up. For all we know, the victim might have been strangulated."

"That would have left marks on her neck," Evie mused.

"Yes, and now that the body is no longer available, we cannot confirm that." The detective shook his head. "Again, I don't wish to give you false hope…"

He stopped for a moment and Evie imagined him measuring his words.

"In the absence of a body, we might quite possibly have an alternative, another way of viewing the body." He looked up. "Some mortuaries make a practice of photographing corpses for their records."

The detective went on to explain he couldn't contact his counterpart at Worthing because it would suggest he was still taking an interest.

"I am trying to find someone who can contact someone already employed at the mortuary." He glanced at Evie. "I'm sure your man of business will come through before then."

Evie sat back and wondered about people who committed murder. "This has to be about gain."

Everyone agreed.

"So, who has the most to gain?"

CHAPTER 21

"Who has the most to gain?" Caro echoed.

"This is going to be a long night." The detective helped himself to some coffee. "In my line of work, we have to consider both the rational and the irrational."

Evie glanced at Tom and smiled. "I believe I'm quite good at coming up with irrational reasons."

"Yes, and I have acquired an appreciation for it," the detective offered.

"This case might require a more outlandish approach," Evie mused. "Money is a great motivator for murder... Assuming we were correct in focusing on Mr. Prentiss and Mr. Addington, it stands to reason they would both have an interest in money. I wish we could discover what Mr. Prentiss offered May Fields. Tom, do you think you could have a chat with the concierge? Find out how May Fields came to work for the hotel. Did she answer an advertisement, did she apply for the job through an agency, or did someone recommend her?"

The detective set his cup down and sat back. "Apart from monetary gain as a reason for murder, we might also consider elimination. As you suggested, May Fields might have known something that made her a liability. But you came up with another interesting idea, which I would like to revisit. You said, we have been assuming the victim was the maid because that's what we were told."

"You want to know if I have anything else to add?" Evie smiled. "I wish I did. I'm afraid it was nothing but a stray thought. Who knows? Something else might come to me in the middle of the night. I might need to let the idea simmer in my mind. Does anyone else have any suggestions?"

"I'm afraid it sounds too far-fetched for me, milady."

Evie laughed. "At the risk of sounding foolish, we have talked about something happening to May Fields between the time she lived and worked at Findon and the time she came to work at the hotel. What if what-ever happened to her was such a momentous event, she had to disappear." Evie jumped to her feet. "Heavens!"

"I believe her ladyship has been struck by another idea," Caro said.

"We were told the victim was May Fields. Tom and I have also been provided with information about May Fields. She was a hard worker and a dreamer. She enjoyed spending her free time daydreaming and pretending to be a grand lady." She strolled across the room, swung around and returned. "We used that information to establish her character. In fact, we have been championing her cause and doing all we can to find justice for her. However..." She stopped again and took a moment to regain her momentum. "What if she found a way to make her dreams come true? We were told she was happy with her circumstances, but what if she wasn't? What if she did something to change her life dramatically? An opportunity presented itself and she could not resist it."

Caro pressed her hands to her cheeks. "She stole a fortune in jewels and money, killed the owner of the fortune, dressed her as a maid and threw her body over the balcony." When Caro finished, she sounded breathless.

Evie lowered herself onto a chair and curled her fingers around the armrest. "She didn't kill someone in the hotel. Otherwise, their absence would have been noted."

"You said it yourself, milady, no one saw her after she entered Mr. Prentiss' room. Working as a maid, she would have known a great deal about the room occupants. She found her prey. A single woman. A wealthy single woman staying at the hotel alone. After May Fields went into the room to replace the soap, she waited a few minutes for the coast to clear. Then, she rushed to another room, most likely a room on the same floor." Caro's voice lowered and became pensive. "She had come to know the woman staying in that room. As I said, a single woman of great wealth. During the night, May Fields killed the woman and hid her body in the wardrobe. Moments after midday when everyone assumed she had taken her half day off, she went into the room which had already been cleaned. She knew she wouldn't be interrupted because the guest staying there was alone. She exchanged her clothes with her and dragged her back to Mr. Prentiss' room. She took her time. By then, she had come to know the Prentiss' routine. They would not return until five in the afternoon. She dragged the body to the room. That's the noise you heard. Then, she used a hose to pour the contents of the brandy into the woman. She then grabbed a brass lamp and smashed her face. Being a maid, she knew how to set the room right. She waited patiently until the right time came. Finally, she positioned the body against the railing and pushed the unfortunate woman off. Then she rushed to the woman's room and assumed her identity. She did this with ease. Remember, Ruth Charles said May Fields enjoyed pretending she was a great lady. To cover her tracks, she wrote a note expressing her wish to be cremated, she sent it to Ruth Charles, her accomplice, who then took care of tying up loose ends..."

One by one, they each drew in a deep breath as if to compensate for the fact they had almost stopped breathing.

Silence settled in the sitting room.

A flash of lightning had them all looking out to sea.

"That looks like a storm heading in," Edmonds said, his voice almost a whisper.

"How can you tell it's coming inland?" Caro asked.

He held up a finger and then pointed toward the

beach as another bolt of lightning flashed across the sky. "That one's closer."

"We might want to think about heading back to the hotel," Caro suggested.

Evie exchanged a raised eyebrow look with Tom and the detective. "Caro?"

"Yes, milady."

"Did you just make all that up?"

"Oh, the story… Did you like it?"

"Yes. I found it intriguing. We all did."

Caro smiled. "I used to tell my brothers bedtime stories. Most of them were scary. They loved them." She shrugged. "Something comes over me and I just get carried away and lose myself in telling the tale."

"You did very well, Caro. We will now have to make further inquiries. Tom."

"Yes, Countess?"

"You will have to ask the concierge if there are any single female guests staying at the hotel."

The detective loosened his tie.

"Detective. You look worried."

"That's because I am. If any of this proves to be correct, then the local police will have a lot of questions to answer."

"Earlier, I told Caro the truth might be staring us in the face, or something along those lines. It is quite possible, someone is close to getting away with murder."

"Not on my watch."

"That's the spirit, detective. I am so glad you came." She turned to Tom. "Now, should we head back?"

"Yes, Richards has offered to drive us back to the hotel."

"We could all do with a good night's sleep, especially if tomorrow springs as many surprises on us as today did."

CHAPTER 22

*S*leep came to Evie in fitful jolts. Her mind remained active throughout the night, refusing to release all the thoughts it had entertained during the day.

As much as she'd liked Caro's idea of May Fields switching places with a wealthy woman, the theory left out the two protagonists Evie had been fixating on.

Unless…

The banker and the lawyer had played a role in the switch, somehow facilitating it…

She peeled an eye open and squinted against the sunlight spilling into her room.

They had a lot to get through that day.

The night before, Tom had walked her to her room and had then returned downstairs to have a word with the concierge. A lot depended on his findings.

Caro had said she would liaise with the maid in the morning and engage her assistance, and Edmonds would be right there to make sure nothing happened to her.

"That leaves me," Evie murmured. She couldn't stand around twiddling her thumbs...

"Good morning, milady." Caro breezed in and went straight to the wardrobe. After a brief perusal, she selected a dress in a soft shade of pink with black stripes on the sleeves and collar. "I hope you slept well." She turned and yelped. "Oh. Oh, you're awake."

"You walk into my room, greet me and then act surprised because I'm awake?"

"I am sincerely surprised. Usually, you shake your head, groan and moan, turn over a couple of times and then, you open your eyes. But here you are, wide awake. I trust you slept well."

"Yes, thank you. There's no use complaining about a restless night. I've been thinking about the day's activities. How sure are we about the maid? What if she somehow assisted May Fields?"

"That's a valid point, milady. But we'll have to take our chances. I'll make sure to stay close to her so she doesn't have the opportunity to alert anyone. We can't abandon the plan now. If the murder weapon is still in the room, we must find it."

"Assuming someone killed the maid before she fell." Evie groaned. "Are we getting carried away?"

"Milady! Please tell me you are not having second thoughts. The detective came all this way to assist you. That has to mean something."

"True."

"If your suspicions did not have any substance, he would not have given you the time of day."

"Also true." Evie flung the bedcovers off and swung her feet off the bed.

"Tom is waiting for you downstairs. He mentioned something about breakfast."

"I suppose I should hurry. I wouldn't want Tom to think I make a habit of taking too long to dress."

Caro laughed under her breath. "I think we are well past that, milady."

When she finished dressing, Evie stepped back and adjusted her hat. "Caro."

"Yes, milady."

"You don't have to do this."

"I would never forgive myself if I didn't do something, milady. Edmonds is hovering nearby, waiting for me. I have already spoken with the maid."

"I thought you weren't going to say anything until you were ready to go into the room. What if she's in on it and alerts her co-conspirators?"

"Relax, milady. When I said Edmonds is hovering nearby, I meant, he is standing guard outside the room she is cleaning."

"I see. You have everything under control. And yet... I'm still not entirely sure about the plan," Evie murmured as she made her way out of her room.

She found Tom in the lobby, his attention fixed on the stairs.

"Have you had a chance to speak with the concierge?" she asked.

"Not yet."

"Where are we going?" she asked as Tom guided her out of the hotel.

"I thought we might have breakfast with the detective."

"You're going to leave Caro and Edmonds?"

"They can look after themselves."

Evie settled into the passenger seat and waited for Tom to climb in before saying, "I'm not sure I will be able to enjoy breakfast while my maid is putting her life at risk."

"I saw the Prentiss couple leave fifteen minutes ago."

"What if they forgot something? Someone should stand guard."

Instead of answering, Tom pulled into traffic and drove as fast as he could, which resulted in a few heads turning.

"You might have warned me to hold onto my hat," Evie exclaimed as he pulled into the drive leading to the Beach House.

He brought the car to a stop right outside the front door.

Coming around to open the passenger door, he said, "You are displaying a great deal of reluctance. I thought you were eager to solve this mystery and see the killer behind bars."

"I am, but not at the expense of my maid."

"Well, we have a busy day ahead. Let's be sensible and have a hearty breakfast."

Richards welcomed them in.

"Good morning, Richards."

He inclined his head. "My lady. The detective is in the library attending to a telephone call."

They followed him through to a dining room facing the sea. Despite not having much of an appetite, Evie helped herself to some eggs and toast.

As she sat down, Tom excused himself. "I'm... I'm going to have a word with the detective."

"B-but, he's on the telephone." Turning, she realized she'd spoken to thin air. Evie huffed out a breath and forced herself to eat. Breaking off a piece of crispy toast, she attacked the egg yolk. It seemed everyone had something to do. "Except me."

The door to the dining room opened and the detective walked in. "Ah, Lady Woodridge. Good morning."

"Good morning, detective. I hope you will join me for breakfast. I am feeling rather abandoned this morning."

He poured himself a cup of coffee and sat opposite Evie. "I have just spoken with your man of business. I must say, I am very impressed. He is a thorough man."

"Yes, Mr. Matthew Keys has been with the family since his youth. He's one of our most trusted employees. What did he have to say?"

"A great deal, my lady. I believe he found answers to all your questions. As I'm not sure why you asked them, I hope you will make sense of them." The detective drew out a notebook. "To start with, Mr. Prentiss has been married two years."

"Oh, yes. Tom and I were wondering about his marital situation. I have never seen such an unhappy looking couple. At one point, we believed they had been roped in or blackmailed to play a role in a conspiracy to commit a crime and that's why they looked so miserable. What else did Mr. Keys say?"

"The Addington couple have also been married for two years."

"Did Mr. Keys manage to find a link between the two men?"

"Yes, and he said he found that to be the most difficult task as the club in question refused to divulge members' details. He eventually succeeded, however, Mr. Keys did not wish to reveal his tactics."

Evie wouldn't be surprised if he had employed bribery. "He is incredibly resourceful."

"As it turns out, our persons of interest both belong to the same club."

"But that doesn't necessarily mean they know each other," Evie said.

"True, however, Mr. Keys' informant confirms the gentlemen have been observed enjoying a drink while sitting by the fireplace."

And, still, that didn't confirm an association between the two men.

The detective smiled. "I believe the following will convince you, my lady. Almost three years ago, Mr. Prentiss drew up a will and handled all estate matters for Mr. Archival Holloway, Mrs. Addington's uncle."

Evie shifted slightly. "I see. Was this, by any chance, before she became Mrs. Addington?"

"Yes, by only a few months. Soon after Mr. Prentiss drew up the will, Mr. Addington met the heiress. A whirlwind romance ensued and they married."

"Are we to assume Mr. Prentiss pointed him in her direction?"

The detective nodded.

"I see. And she just happened to be an heiress."

"As I've often said, coincidences tend to expire at some point." He turned a couple of pages on his notebook. "I believe you came up with a theory about wealthy widows."

"Yes, we thought they might have been targeting them. And now Caro has come up with an equally enthralling theory. I must say, she has impressed me."

The butler refreshed Evie's coffee. Taking a sip, she mused, "Maybe that's what the maid overheard. Mr. Prentiss might have been talking about it with his wife, telling her Mr. Addington married not for love but rather for money. That is not the sort of information you wish to have spread around. If the maid overheard it, she might have decided to use it against Mr. Addington to extort money from him." She shook her head. "I'm afraid all the different theories we have contrived are currently meshing inside my head. I fear I might never be able to entertain another clear thought again." She looked over her shoulder. "Tom seems to have disappeared."

"He mentioned something about talking to the concierge."

"Aha! He has abandoned me. This is his way of keeping me out of the line of fire. Just as well, I'm sure I would have been a hindrance. Everyone had a task except me."

They heard hurried footsteps approaching. A moment later, Caro burst into the room.

"Milady. What an adventure we've had."

"Caro! I'm ever so happy to see you alive and well. Do sit down and have a cup of tea."

"I'm far too excited for that." She looked toward the door. Edmonds appeared carrying a bulky object. "We have absconded with a statue!"

CHAPTER 23

*E*vie glanced at the detective. "I'm sure Caro didn't mean what she said…"

"Oh, yes. I did. I stole a statue from the hotel," Caro stated. She could not have sounded prouder.

Evie tried to signal with her eyes, but Caro either ignored her or she felt compelled to throw caution to the wind.

"As a matter of fact, I also helped myself to a pillow case. Show them, Edmonds."

Evie sighed and watched Edmonds set the bulky object on the table. Taking care to only handle the pillow case, he unveiled the statue.

Caro grinned. "We actually changed our tactics at the last minute. While I engaged the maids in conversation, Edmonds sneaked into the room and grabbed the statue. We had discussed this earlier in the morning. I noticed the table lamp had a glass top and a cord attached, so I concluded it could not have been used as a weapon." Pointing at the statue, she added, "I haven't actually wiped it, so it might all have been for naught." Caro dug inside her handbag, produced a white handkerchief and handed it to the detective.

The butler jumped into action and put a jug of water and a small dish on the table. Clearly, he had heard the detective's story the previous night.

Drawing in a deep breath, the detective dampened the handkerchief and began to dab the statue, paying particular attention to the ridges.

Evie studied the dancing girl, casting an appreciative eye over the stylized design. To think it might have ended someone's life or rather contributed to the end of a life.

The detective stopped dabbing the statue and held the handkerchief out for their inspection.

Caro gasped and pressed her hands to her cheeks. "Is that... Is that blood?"

"It appears to be." The detective smiled at her and then at Evie. "Ladies, gentlemen, I believe we have our murder weapon."

And no victim, Evie couldn't help thinking. She shifted and found a chair to sit on. "Amazing. What now?"

The door to the dining room opened and Tom walked in.

"Just in time," Evie said and pointed to the handkerchief.

As he studied it, he said, "I spoke with the concierge. May Fields applied for the position herself." He looked straight at Evie when he added, "This happened straight after Mr. Prentiss' visit to Findon."

He did not wait for their responses. "Also, only one guest left before her scheduled departure."

"A woman?" Evie asked.

He nodded and handed the detective a piece of paper. "I wrote down her London address. It would be worth following up on it. Although..." he raked his fingers through his hair, "What are the chances? I mean, really? What are the chances? All along, we've been thinking of May Fields as the victim and she could, quite possibly, now be the killer. I... I... My apologies, I am lost for words."

"Does this mean our other suspects are off the hook?" Evie asked.

"I think it means we are a step closer to proving one possibility," the detective offered. "But you proposed another scenario, Lady Woodridge." The detective took care to cover the statue. "This will need to be analyzed. The killer did a thorough job of cleaning it, but not thorough enough." He pushed out a breath. "This gives rise to more questions than I could ever answer."

"Will you speak with your Worthing counterpart?" Evie asked.

"No, I'm afraid not. At this stage, I think I will need to go straight to Scotland Yard." He looked up at the butler. "Do you have something I could use as a carry bag? I will be catching the next train to London."

"Will you return here, detective?" Evie asked.

"Quite possibly." He nodded and then shook his head. "I have no idea how I am going to explain all this."

"I certainly don't envy you, detective." Evie tapped

her chin in thought. "I keep going over everything we have put together and all I can see are loose ends. Mr. Prentiss' visit to Findon and subsequent contact with May Fields. That is a coincidence we cannot overlook. His association with Mr. Addington is another one. The emergence of a note written by May Fields. Why didn't Ruth Charles mention it when we visited Findon? I'm sure I told her I had offered to take care of the arrangements."

"We'll get to the bottom of it, Lady Woodridge. Now, I will have to take my leave. I promise to contact you when I know something."

"That is very considerate, detective. Thank you."

"It's the least I can do, my lady."

"This almost feels anticlimactic," Evie mused as they made their way back to the hotel.

"Would you care to take a drive? It might clear your head," Tom offered.

"Oh, yes. I like the idea of escaping from it all…"

He made a turn and headed in the opposite direction.

"I take it you know where you are going."

"Brighton. It's not far from here, which makes me wonder why you chose Worthing as our destination."

"Oh, it was nothing more than a coincidence. Caro expressed a desire to visit the seaside and I received an invitation to stay at the hotel." Evie laughed. "I believe I am about to launch into another scenario. After all, what are the chances of receiving such an offer right at the time when my maid expresses a desire to visit a seaside town?"

"Are you about to suggest the hotel owner planned it all?"

"That would be too far-fetched." She lowered her hat over her eyes. "What should I look forward to seeing in Brighton?"

"Great architecture."

"Oh."

"The area has a significant Stone Age history."

"More flint mines?"

Tom laughed. "No, I don't think so. There is a pier."

"Oh, heavens."

"By the way, the concierge said he saw Mr. Prentiss arrive soon before five on the afternoon of the incident. He and his wife went straight to the library."

That placed Mr. Prentiss downstairs. "I suppose he made a point of making sure the concierge knew that."

"Yes, he asked if the newspapers were up to date."

She turned her attention to the sea. The storm had passed, taking all the clouds away with it and leaving them with a bright blue sky.

Evie revisited their latest theory.

Caro had opened their eyes to an unexpected scenario. She tried to picture May Fields' first days working at the hotel. Had she been in awe of all the ladies parading around? While everyone had described May Fields as a down-to-earth hard worker, Evie knew a person's attitude and outlook could change and evolve into something entirely different.

She could see May Fields thinking how nice it would be to enjoy staying at the hotel as a guest rather than spending her days cleaning the rooms.

What would it take?

The words drummed inside her head. Evie closed her eyes and watched a scene unfold in her mind...

In the process of doing her job, May Fields entered a room occupied by a young woman. Evie pictured May looking inside the wardrobe and admiring all the beautiful gowns. While she worked, she might have imagined staying at the hotel as a guest. Later, she learned from the other maids the woman was unmarried and quite wealthy. A seed was planted in her mind. She wondered what it would be like to step into her shoes...

Everyone working at the hotel knew Evie was the Countess of Woodridge. What could a maid learn about her from her belongings? Evie chose to travel light. She had a notebook with essential emergency contact names and telephone numbers. In her opinion, no one would be able to sketch out an entire life from the few possessions she carried with her.

Her granny, on the other hand, always carried with her framed photographs which she scattered about whichever room she happened to be staying at, to make the place look cozy, she'd often said.

Her granny also traveled with a satchel containing important documents she couldn't bear to leave behind. They were all copies of the originals. If anyone cared to look through them, they would discover just how wealthy she was...

Something must have alerted May Fields to the guest's single status, Evie thought. Perhaps the unsuspecting guest kept a journal where she'd written all her innermost thoughts, including information about being alone in the world. Or... Attending yet another funeral. Seeing her relatives disappear, one by one until she was the only one left.

In Evie's scenario, May Fields had seen the opportunity and she'd taken it. She'd spent some time working out a plot, ironing out the details until she could be sure it would work.

Then, on the fateful day, she killed the old May Fields and was reborn as a wealthy single woman, free to do as she pleased.

How would she have gone about stealing the rest of the other woman's life and identity? Evie's mind turned to practical matters. She would've had to gain access to her bank account. That could be a complicated matter. Most wealthy people had their money tied up in investments as well as an entourage of people employed to look after their affairs...

Frowning, Evie opened her eyes and sat up.

"As much as I love Caro's idea, I don't think May Fields could have pulled it off by herself."

Tom leaned in and Evie had to repeat herself.

Changing gears, he brought the roadster to a stop.

"Have we arrived?" Evie looked around but couldn't see anything that resembled a resort town.

"No, I just wanted to give you my full attention. Run that idea by me again."

Evie explained her scenario and finished by saying

she didn't believe May Fields would have the knowledge to pull off such a complicated crime. "Think about all the people I employ to make sure my possessions and money are well taken care of. They will immediately realize she is an impostor." She adjusted her hat and shifted to face him. "Let's assume the woman had a considerable amount of money with her, May Fields thinks she can take it and go somewhere else, some place where no one will recognize her. The money won't last and someone will realize the woman is missing. Yes, she's lost all her relatives, but there must be others who would notice her absence."

"Maybe May Fields didn't think it all through."

"Maybe, but something tells me she would have been thorough." What were they missing?

"And?" Tom prompted her.

Shrugging, Evie said, "Perhaps we should continue on to Brighton. I'm all out of ideas." Evie tried to clear her mind of her obsessions. She leaned toward Tom and said, "By the way, thank you for contacting Detective Inspector O'Neill."

The matter was now in the hands of someone who would stop at nothing to get to the truth. She straightened her skirt. In her efforts to update her wardrobe, she appeared to have made some odd choices. Either that or she simply needed to become accustomed to wearing dresses with large blocks of color... and hats with fruit.

The roadster slowed down snapping Evie out of her reverie.

"Here we are. Brighton."

"You were right. It has a pier."

Tom smiled. "Would you care to take a walk along it?"

"I feel we must. Otherwise, I'll never hear the end of it. I should tell Caro to drive down with Edmonds. This pier seems to be larger than the one at Worthing."

"I believe there is a theater, paddle steamer excursions, military bands and even daredevil high divers."

"If Caro comes, and I'm sure she will, we'll never be able to tear her away. She'll insist I uproot my life and move to Brighton."

They managed to walk to the end of the pier without once bringing up the subject of May Fields. Evie had to bite her lip only twice to stop herself from talking about the case.

Tom seemed to be content to whistle under his breath. The tune had, by now, become quite familiar.

"What is the name of that song?"

Tom smiled. "Seaside Trippers. Catchy, isn't it?"

"Yes, I'm sure I'll be humming it in my sleep tonight."

After a moment of silence, Tom said, "I believe you have just set a record. You have gone a full half hour without once mentioning the case."

"I have been working on strengthening my will-power. It's almost within my grasp, if only…"

"If only I hadn't brought up the subject?"

"Well, yes. In fact, now that you have mentioned it, I've been thinking. Why did May Fields choose that room? Why not spare herself the trouble of dragging the body to Mr. Prentiss' room?"

"Because she needed the body to fall from another room," Tom suggested.

"Oh, clearly that half hour of not talking about the subject has made me rusty. Yes, you have a point."

Tom resumed his whistling.

"Actually, we seem to have forgotten about Mr. Prentiss. I'm still curious to know what sort of job he offered her." Evie clicked her fingers. "Remember our theory about the wealthy widow?"

"Yes."

"Well, my mind is entertaining ideas about impersonating someone. That's what we assume May Fields did. What if Mr. Prentiss traveled to Findon on business and when he saw May Fields he thought she reminded him of someone. An idea sparked in his mind."

Tom stopped and looked at her. "He asked her to pretend to be someone else?"

"Yes."

CHAPTER 24

a seagull squawked. Turning, Evie saw a couple on the edge of the pier using a tidbit to entice the bird into coming closer.

The sound of laughter swirled around them. Children ran and played. She saw a line forming outside the theater.

Shaking off the distractions, she said, "Caro found a statue with what will most likely turn out to be the victim's blood. However, the body is no longer available so the police will not be able to make comparisons. Something happened in that room and Mr. Prentiss has to be a part of it."

"Evie."

"Yes?"

"Take a deep breath. You are tripping over your words."

Evie pressed her hand to her chest. She felt her breath coming hard and fast. She knew they'd missed something. Something essential. She'd told Caro it had been staring them in the face...

"We should head back to Worthing."

"Are you sure? Wouldn't you like to have lunch here?"

"Lunch? I couldn't eat a bite." She pushed out a breath. She had done enough. In fact, more than enough. Now, the matter was in the hands of the authorities... Her shoulders lowered. "Yes, I suppose we should stop somewhere. Although, I fail to understand your obsession with eating."

Tom laughed. "I think it will do you a world of good to slow down."

True. Yet she remained eager to return to Worthing and contact the detective who might actually have some news for them.

They chose the first restaurant they came across. Evie sat down and drew out her notebook. "I need to get some of these ideas down otherwise I might scream."

"Would you like me to order for you?"

"Yes, please." She shook her head. "It cannot possibly be a coincidence that Mr. Prentiss and Mr. Addington both found their way to Worthing. I don't recall seeing them engaging in conversation which, in itself, is odd and points at some sort of duplicity." Evie stopped only briefly when the waiter came by their table to take their order. "As for Mr. Prentiss having an alibi... Well, that's just nonsense. In my opinion, he arrived at the hotel in time to throw the victim from the balcony. Just because he's been placed at the library doesn't mean he didn't find a way to rush upstairs and... The back stairs. Of course. The concierge saw him going into the library, but Mr. Prentiss could just as easily have taken the back stairs to run upstairs and complete his mission."

Tom glanced up at the waiter who'd been doing his best to pretend he hadn't heard a single word Evie had said.

To her surprise, Tom ordered sandwiches and requested that they be wrapped up.

"I guess we'll be eating on the run," he said.

"But... why?"

"While I appreciate your efforts, I couldn't bear to see you suffer in silence."

Evie gave him a bright smile. "Oh, you are wonderfully understanding."

Within minutes, they were on the road and headed back to Worthing. Evie leaned in close to Tom and spoke at the top of her voice so Tom could hear her over the roar of the engine. "I just know there is something obvious we are missing."

Tom nodded and took a bite of his sandwich.

"What is the first thing I do whenever we return to the hotel?"

"You go upstairs to change."

"Precisely." Evie could tell by his glance he hadn't quite grasped the meaning of her revelation. "The concierge told you Mr. Prentiss and his wife returned to the hotel and went straight to the library. Why didn't Mrs. Prentiss go upstairs to change?"

"Because she and her husband knew a murder was about to take place."

"Yes!" But she still maintained Mr. Prentiss had used the back stairs to dash up to the room.

Tom took another bite of his sandwich. "Have I mentioned you have developed an obsessive streak?" he asked.

Evie grinned. "Maybe. Once or twice." Evie kept shifting and stretching her neck to try and catch sight of Worthing. Finally, she saw a familiar building. "We're here."

"Yes, we have arrived." Tom slowed down and turned into the street leading up to the Beach House. "If you can bear the delay, I thought we might stop at the house and see if there are any messages from your man of business or the detective."

"Good idea. You do seem to come up with them just at the right time." When he stopped the roadster, she didn't wait for him to open the passenger door. Jumping out, Evie hurried to the front door, but before she reached it, the front door opened.

"My lady," the butler greeted her.

When he stepped aside to let her in, Evie said, "Hello Richards, are there any messages for us?"

"I'm afraid not, my lady."

Thanking him, she turned and crashed into Tom. "No messages," she said rubbing her nose. "We should head back to the hotel."

"Because..."

"That's where all the action is. Surely..."

Looking over her shoulder, Tom smiled at Richards.

"Lady Woodridge wishes to return to the hotel. Thank you, Richards. I'm sure we'll have reason to return later on."

"As you wish, sir."

As they climbed back into the roadster, Tom mused, "I could have sworn you got your brightest ideas during moments of quiet introspection. I don't know where I got that impression from."

"What's wrong, Tom? Are you having trouble keeping up with me?"

"Actually," he straightened his tie. "I feel the leash might be back on."

Evie laughed. "I'll try not to tug too hard."

Tom wove his way through traffic and pulled into a side street where he found a place for the motor car.

"Would it make any difference if I suggested blending in?" Tom asked as they made their way to the hotel.

"What do you mean?"

"Everyone is strolling by at a leisurely pace and here we are hurrying along. Actually, you're trotting and I'm lengthening my stride. But I feel you are about to break into a run. People are noticing."

"Yes, I suppose you're right. We wouldn't want to start a riot." Evie forced herself to slow down.

When they entered the hotel, her gaze skated around the lobby to try to locate any of the protagonists in the unfolding drama.

"I don't see any of them around," she said, her voice heavy with urgency. "Not even Caro and Edmonds." In her eyes, everyone looked suspicious. The man behind the front desk looked up and held her gaze. The bellboy turned and looked at her only to look away quickly. She could have sworn a man reading a newspaper peered at her only to lift the newspaper when she met his gaze. And... and a woman stood a few feet away, holding a compact mirror. She adjusted it as if to catch Evie's reflection.

Suddenly, the place was swarming with suspicious characters.

"Caro and Edmonds are most likely making the best of their vacation." Tom checked his watch. "As for the others, they're either having a late lunch or they're out and about enjoying their final moments of freedom."

"Tom! Are you teasing me?"

"I wouldn't dream of it, Countess."

"Wait here for me, please. As long as we're here, I might as well go upstairs and change. Oh, and remind me never to wear pink again. I think it makes me rather erratic."

She rushed up the main staircase. Out of the corner of her eye, she saw Tom heading toward the library. He had been right about one thing, Evie thought. She did rather enjoy her quiet moments of rumination and appeared to do her best thinking when left alone.

Reaching her room, she decided she actually did her best thinking when bouncing off ideas with Tom or Caro...

In this instance, however, she did need to spend some time alone with her thoughts. There were simply too many of them.

Once inside her room, she changed dresses, opting

for her favorite shade of pale green and then sat at her dresser to think.

If May Fields had stolen a guest's identity, the police would catch up with her. Evie made a mental note to tell the detective Mrs. Johnstone from Findon had a photograph of May Fields. That would help to identify the woman and Mrs. Johnstone would surely be able to pick her out of a crowd, even if she was dressed as a lady.

How else could they reveal her real identity?

Evie studied her fingernails. Over the summer, she had spent a lot of time working in her little patch of garden. Yet, her fingers didn't show any signs of being put to work. Would someone who'd been working in service show signs…?

Evie brushed her hands across her face. She really needed to put it all to rest and let the police do their job.

Startled by the sound of a hard thump, Evie at first tried to ignore it, but the propensity to satisfy her curiosity won out.

Evie held her breath for a moment and strained to hear more sounds. When that didn't work, she got up and edged toward the open window. Anyone who saw her would think she wanted to eavesdrop. The edge of Evie's lip kicked up as she thought they would be correct.

She leaned out. Looking up at the floor above, she saw the curtain billowing out. A moment later, she heard a murmured discussion. But despite her efforts, she could not make any of it out.

Stepping back, she walked around her room, mouthing some of the words she thought she'd heard. "Mess? Miss?" She could feel herself sliding right back into her obsession about the case.

Evie stopped in the middle of the room. This had gone far enough. She had taken a game and turned it into a hunt for a real killer. Now there was nothing more for her to do.

Giving a firm nod, she went downstairs telling herself no one got away with murder.

When she reached the lobby, she looked up and saw a couple of men dressed in gray suits standing by the entrance to the hotel. Something about them set them apart from all the hotel guests she'd been seeing on a regular basis. They looked alert. Determined. Definitely not at ease.

They scanned the lobby with such intensity, Evie felt they were looking for someone.

Hurrying across the lobby, she headed toward the library where she knew she would find Tom.

Before disappearing down the hallway leading to the library, she slowed down. Evie looked over her shoulder and toward the entrance. The two men were staring straight at her.

Evie backed away until she lost sight of them. Turning, she dashed toward the library where she found Tom sitting by the window reading a newspaper.

"Tom. There you are."

"Yes, I've been here all along. Oh, I beg your pardon. I suppose you expected me to wait in the lobby."

She sat down next to him and grabbed hold of his

arm. "There are..." Frowning, she turned toward the opposite corner and saw a familiar face. Mr. Addington. She looked back at Tom and whispered. "Mr. Addington?"

"Yes," he whispered back. "What were you going to say?"

"Oh... There are..." She heard someone else entering. Turning, she saw Mr. Prentiss making a beeline for a chair by the fireplace. There were two chairs near Mr. Addington, yet Mr. Prentiss chose to sit elsewhere.

"Evie?"

Out of the corner of her eye, she saw someone else walking in.

Mrs. Prentiss.

She walked toward a bookcase and stopped to peruse the books.

Evie kept her attention peeled on the woman and said in a soft murmur, "There are two men standing in the lobby. I think they're policemen."

"What makes you think so?"

"Well, they looked rather suspicious, in a good sort of way."

Tom set his newspaper down. "Would you like to take a stroll before dinner, which will of course require another change of clothes?"

"I've never heard you complain about that."

"And I wasn't complaining now. However, I've only now noticed just how many times you change your outfits."

"It's not me... It's expected."

"Yes, of course."

"So, what do you suppose brought the police here?"

"They must be closing in on a suspect," he suggested.

"So soon? We've been here nearly a week and we've been going around in circles."

He smiled. "Isn't that what amateurs usually do?"

She settled back in her chair. "I think I'd like to stay here. I have a feeling something is about to happen." She straightened her skirt and glanced up in time to see Mrs. Addington enter.

"Strange. I didn't hear her walk in," Evie whispered.

"That's because she came in from the other door." Tom gestured toward the end of a bookcase.

Evie leaned slightly and saw a door. "I keep forgetting about that back door." She watched Mrs. Addington settle beside her husband. Evie tried to get a good look at her face but Mrs. Addington sat at an angle. "It just occurred to me. We're sitting in a library."

"Yes, but I'm afraid it doesn't compare to your library. The books are aimed at light reading."

Crossing her legs, Evie continued to study Mrs. Addington. She remembered bumping into her a couple of days before. Something about her had struck her as odd.

She clicked her fingers and tried to remember her first impressions of the woman.

She thought she'd worn too much rouge on her cheeks and had laughed too loudly. Also, there had been something uncouth about her...

Evie curled her fingers around Tom's arm. "Tom." She leaned in and whispered. "Have a good look at Mrs. Addington."

CHAPTER 25

*E*vie nudged Tom with her elbow.

"I'm looking. I'm looking"

"Yes, but are you seeing what I'm seeing?"

"I'll need to decipher that first."

"Try to picture her without the hat and the rouge."

"Is there anything else you'd like me to take off her?"

Evie gave him another nudge with her elbow. "Am I imagining it? Yes, of course, I'm imagining it. It can't be true. Can you picture May Fields as Mrs. Addington?"

"That photograph Mrs. Johnstone showed us… Well, I didn't want to say it then and I'm reluctant to say it now."

"What?"

"It looked grainy."

"Yes, but can you see the shape of the face? I think it's the same as May Fields' and I've probably noticed it now because Mrs. Addington is not laughing. Every time we've seen Mrs. Addington, she was laughing and that tends to distort the face. She's looking down, but I'm sure her face is the same shape as May Fields'. Can you see it?"

Her gaze strayed to the door leading to the back stairs. "You said the concierge saw Mr. Prentiss come into the library just before five. Do you think he might have used the back stairs to go up and throw the dead body off the balcony? I know I suggested it before, but now I think it might really be the only way he could have done it."

"Am I done looking?"

"You're still looking but you're also thinking about the back stairs."

"Fine. Yes, I can juggle the two."

Evie watched Mr. and Mrs. Prentiss cross the room, their expressions as morose as ever.

She checked her watch. It was too early to change for dinner. "Where do you suppose they're going?"

Tom chortled. "You just had to sneak another task in. Would you like to follow them? After I try to figure out if Mr. Prentiss used the back stairs and if the woman I'm looking at is really May Fields..." He straightened. "Hang on. I'm beginning to see the resemblance."

The sound of a commotion just outside the library had them both turning.

"That sounds like Caro." Evie surged to her feet. Two people walked into the library, or rather, they backed into the library.

Mr. and Mrs. Prentiss.

They were being herded back into the library by one of the two men Evie had seen standing by the hotel door.

"What is going on here?" Evie murmured.

A moment later, Caro and Edmonds appeared, the other man wearing a gray suit a step behind them.

"Milady." Caro rushed toward her. "You wouldn't believe it. That man wouldn't let us leave the hotel. Not even when I mentioned I worked for you. He dragged us in here. What is happening?"

"I asked that just a second ago, Caro." Evie gestured to the chairs beside Tom. "I guess you should both make yourselves comfortable."

Mr. and Mrs. Addington both surged to their feet and turned toward the door leading to the back stairs only to bump into another man in a gray suit.

"If I didn't know better, I'd think we are being sequestered." Evie turned to Tom and found him still staring at Mrs. Addington. His eyes narrowed and then widened.

Evie said. "Now you see the resemblance?"

"Yes. She turned and you were right about her not laughing. Do you really think it's May Fields?"

Evie wondered what would happen if she called out her name. How would they react? Would Mr. Addington pull out a revolver?

"Don't," Tom said almost as if he'd read her thoughts. "They might be armed.

"But we have to do something about it." Evie looked over her shoulder. The men in gray were standing by the door. "Caro. Did they identify themselves?"

"Oh, yes. Didn't I mention it? They showed us their police identification badges. Do you think we are now suspects?"

Tom and Evie exchanged a look that spoke of surprise. "Us? But we've been assisting the police."

Caro grinned. "Thereby giving yourselves the perfect alibis."

Across the room, Mr. Addington appeared to be holding a heated conversation with the man who had prevented him and his wife from leaving the library.

"I'd like to know what that's all about." The door to the library opened and a man walked in. "Detective Inspector O'Neill," Evie exclaimed.

He stopped to talk with the policeman in the gray suit then turned to face everyone in the library.

Seeing Evie and Tom, he nodded and cleared his throat. "If I could please have your attention. Firstly, I would like to apologize for this rather unorthodox setting. I have asked that you all remain here because I needed to ask a few questions and wished to do so without any formalities."

Mr. Prentiss stepped forward. "Now, see here…"

"You must be Mr. Prentiss," the detective said, his voice amiable.

Evie gasped and whispered, "I think the detective is going to solve the murder and we are here to witness it all."

"I should like to ask Mrs. Prentiss a question."

The woman gave a half-hearted nod.

"On the day of the unfortunate incident when a

maid fell over a balcony, what time did you return to the hotel?"

Mrs. Prentiss answered with confidence. "Just before five o'clock. I believe the concierge can verify that."

The detective asked the others the same question. Everyone had returned to the hotel just before five o'clock.

The detective then spent the next few minutes asking each guest to retrace their steps after five o'clock.

"It was a ghastly business," Mr. Addington said. "My wife was greatly upset by it all."

"Mr. Addington, is this your first time to Worthing?"

"I fail to see what that has to do with anything."

"I am merely curious to know why you chose this place for your vacation."

"A friend recommended it."

The detective brushed his hand across his chin. "A final vacation by the seaside before you sail to America? I sometimes can't help but feel envious."

Evie's fingers tightened around Tom's arm. "Did you hear that?" she whispered.

Mr. Addington paled.

"We have been making a few inquiries. It seems you have closed up your London house and transferred all your business interests. It looks to me like you were thinking of leaving and never returning." He looked at Mrs. Addington. "How do you feel about that, Mrs. Addington?"

The woman lifted her chin slightly. "I am very pleased with my husband's plans."

"You recently inherited a vast fortune from your uncle. I believe he was your last living relative."

"Y-yes."

"My condolences." The detective looked down at the ground for a moment. "You don't mind leaving London and sailing away?"

She nodded.

"I suppose that means you have changed your mind about divorcing your husband."

Evie gasped and whispered, "That's it. She wanted to divorce her husband so he arranged to kill her."

"Milady. I think that's one of the scenarios you came up with."

"Oh, I don't think so…"

Instead of pursuing his line of questioning with Mrs. Addington, the detective turned to Mr. Prentiss. "You traveled to Findon earlier in the year for business."

"I had to deal with an estate matter."

"There you were surprised to encounter a young woman who looked strikingly familiar. When you returned to London, you went to see your friend, Mr. Addington and told him about May Fields' striking resemblance to his wife, the wife who had recently inherited a vast fortune and now wanted to divorce him. The woman you had introduced him to after drawing up her uncle's will."

Both men protested.

Mrs. Prentiss swayed and fainted while Mrs.

Addington forgot herself and slumped down on a chair, her face in her hands.

Evie then realized they had been preoccupied with Mr. Prentiss' comings and goings but had overlooked Mr. Addington.

"Mr. Addington. On the day a young woman died here at the hotel, you and your wife made your way downstairs. It was just after midday. You took the back stairs and instead of going all the way to the lobby, you went to Mr. Prentiss' room. A maid opened the door for you and your wife. You then proceeded to kill your wife and you smashed her face until it was unrecognizable. Then, you and the maid who had by then dressed as your wife, left the hotel and went out to lunch."

Mr. Addington stood speechless.

Evie expected him to at least call for his lawyer, but he didn't.

"We know Mr. Prentiss made sure to have an alibi for his precise whereabouts, but you didn't."

Mr. Addington's fingers curled into the palms of his hands. Evie could see his teeth clenching and his eyes narrowing.

"You returned to the hotel later that afternoon with the woman pretending to be your wife. You cleaned the scene of the crime and at just after five o'clock, you pushed your wife off the balcony. Then, you made your way downstairs where you mingled with the hotel guests."

Mr. Addington exploded. "Nonsense."

"Yes, I thought you might say that." The detective turned and signaled to one of the police officers standing by the door. He opened the door and someone stepped inside.

Evie couldn't see the person's face because the detective blocked her view but in the next instant, she heard the woman gasp.

"May. My dear. You're alive."

"*R*ight under our noses." Evie shook her head. The answer had been so simple. Once they'd suspected May Fields of faking her death and taking over someone else's identity, they should have remembered Mrs. Johnstone.

The police had put everyone in handcuffs and taken them away, leaving Evie to discuss what they'd just witnessed with the others.

"To think," Caro said, "if you hadn't been bored with your trip to the seaside, you would never have thought of suspecting anyone."

Evie grinned. "I'm sure it had something to do with the police not wanting to question us."

Tom laughed. "You really took exception to that."

The detective walked into the library. Shaking his head, he sat down.

"Congratulations, detective," Evie said.

"Thank you, my lady. Now we have the hard task of putting together a solid case against them. Your man of business was extremely helpful, providing us with the pertinent information which tied everything up for us, including information about Mr. Addington making travel arrangements. It appears they were planning on making their escape within a few days and Ruth Charles was going to join them in America as a reward for her part in the conspiracy. Your man of business even found Mrs. Addington's maid who told him about her wish to seek a divorce. I had been in the middle of trying to process all the information he'd sourced when I remembered you mentioning Mrs. Johnstone. If we were to prove your suspicions correct, we needed someone to identify May Fields."

"Has she said anything yet?" Evie asked.

"She's claiming her life had been threatened by Mr. Prentiss if she didn't co-operate. Ruth Charles has been apprehended. She will need to answer charges of conspiring to murder. I believe they will all turn on each other but the harshest penalty will befall Mr. Addington for striking the fatal blow."

"So, this was all about money and greed," Evie murmured.

"Yes."

"Oh, what about the guest who left before her scheduled departure? The one I thought May Fields might have killed."

"She has been located, safe and sound." The detective smiled. "I rather enjoyed Caro's theory."

"Yes, we all did," Evie said. "I just don't understand why they lingered at the hotel for so long. I realize they might have been trying to avoid suspicion, but an early departure would have been justified. I remember thinking if someone had died in my room, I would have requested another room. In hindsight, I believe I would have simply left early."

The detective nodded. "That was definitely a mistake on their part. Clearly, they were confident of getting away with murder." The detective dug inside his coat pocket. "I have a photograph from the mortuary." He took it out and slipped it back in. "There is no point in showing it. I doubt anyone could have recognized the victim from the photograph. The damage to the face was quite severe."

They all fell silent.

A waiter came in carrying a tray of tea and coffee.

"Will you join us, detective?"

"Thank you, my lady." He helped himself to a cup of tea. As he stirred in some sugar, he smiled. "I just informed Detective Inspector Hopper about the key role you played in finding the killer."

Tom laughed under his breath. "You robbed Lady Woodridge of the pleasure of seeing his reaction."

"My apologies. I wish I could have been more accommodating," the detective said.

"I'm not complaining, inspector. At least you allowed us to remain here while you wrapped up this case."

"Yes, that was rather unusual. I considered sending in a note requesting that you leave the library."

"Oh, I'm so glad you didn't."

"Will you be sharing your travel tales with the dowager?" the detective asked.

"I would hardly know where to begin."

Tom smiled at Evie. "Do I need to refresh your memory? Let me see... You'd been quite bored with the idea of being at the seaside, something I'm sure the dowager would empathize with."

She laughed. "I was not. I merely needed some time to... find my sea legs."

The detective set his teacup down. "I take it you will remain here for the rest of the week."

"Yes, I have to walk on the beach barefoot and build a sand castle... Oh and collect some seashells. Yes, I feel I should take something tangible back with me. Proof that I have spent my time wisely... minding my own business..."

AUTHOR NOTES - FACTS AND HISTORICAL REFERENCES

All care has been taken to remain historically correct. Normally, I include a list of words or phrases which had been in use well before the 1920s. This time, however, I am only including one.

Top drawer: The drawer in question here is the highest drawer of a bedroom chest of drawers. This was where the gentry kept their most valuable items: jewelry, best clothes etc. The phrase 'top-drawer' was initially used to denote a person's level of social standing, based on their family background. The earliest citation of the phrase comes from the English writer Horace Vachell, in the novel The Hill, a Romance of Friendship, 1905

Made in the USA
Las Vegas, NV
12 June 2022

50138288R00142